Battle For

Rumora

By
Mac Fortner

DISCLAIMER

Dedication

Thanks to my wife Cindy, who is always there to lend her support and love.

This is book two of the Sunny Ray Series. Be sure to pick up book one– Rum City Bar

Don't miss the Cam Derringer series–Knee Deep–out now. Book two from Cam Derringer–Bloodshot–out soon.

MAC FORTNER

RUMORA

Out on the ocean, under the sun
Sailing with you, and drinking rum
And having too much fun, just being here

Watching the sunset, from a tropical isle
Beats the snow, by a country mile
And you know, it makes me smile
Love the music I hear

Sail away with me, in the moonlight
We'll navigate, by the stars at night
Until, we're out of sight
And they fade away
Sail away with me, to Rumora Bay

We'll drink our rum out in the sand
Every island is our promise land
Just take me by the hand
And we'll fade away
Sail away with me to Rumora Bay

Sail away with me, in the moonlight
We'll navigate, by the stars at night
Until, we're out of sight
And they fade away
Sail away with me, to Rumora Bay

Mac Fortner

MAC FORTNER

Battle for Rumora

PROLOGUE

I WAS SITTING in Rum City Bar, playing my old guitar, the first time I met Captain Louis Lewis. It was a tranquil, peaceful, if not magical morning. I was on the island, which I owned, sitting at the bar, which I owned, thinking about how lucky I was to have all this and good friends too.

1

Not just friends who came around because you can give them the pleasures of life, although I have a few of those too, but real friends, who would put their life on the line for me. My friends have.

My name is Sunny Ray. I'm six foot two and one hundred ninety five pounds. I have blond hair that some consider a little on the long side. I became a country music star two years ago and it's been a wild ride.

My first song *Rum City Bar* was quite a hit. It gave me the opportunity to tour with Billie Jay Player, one of the biggest stars that country music has ever seen. I learned many things from him, including humbleness.

I had the island to myself today, after just returning from a two-month tour. I was still trying to unwind from all the excitement, women screaming every time I came out on stage, the constant beating of the drums behind me. There was a lot of adrenalin flowing on the stage.

Rum City Bar is the name on the sign over my dock. This was my dream come true, a place where I can sing and party with my friends. The bar has done well. We are only open on Friday through Sunday and it is packed.

I have a stunning panoramic view of the Gulf of Mexico and the island is thick in vegetation. Some is natural, but most was planted here when we built the bar and sound studio. My apartment is above the studio and I spend as much time here as I can.

It's a beautiful island located just south of Marathon Key, Florida. You can't find it if you don't know where to look. We planned it that way. It's a magical little piece of land. Some folks who have visited it, say their whole life changed. They say they feel lighter inside and see things differently, with more feeling.

I actually fell in love with the keys the first time I saw them. I knew this would be the life for me.

Situated in the middle of the island, my bar has a scenic view in every direction. It has no walls, so the only way we can close it, is to close the entire island. I love spending time here alone, but when I have several hundred, or a thousand guests, I love it too.

I looked down at the hamburgers I was grilling and flipped them. They had sear marks on this side now. Just looking at them makes me hungry. Then I looked back out at the ocean.

I was watching the billowing sails of a great schooner, which was lazily tacking back and forth in the wind, working its way toward my island. I first spotted it on the horizon about forty-five minutes ago. Now it was only a mile or less away and I could see the strong lines and mammoth masts holding tight the full sails, which captured the wind and pushed the vessel onward. I wondered what exotic destination it was in search of and what magical journey it has come from.

The sails collapsed once more, as the great ship turned, losing for a moment the wind it held for precious fuel, and searched for another gust. Then the sails filled again and the bow raised as it accelerated.

I checked the burgers again and picked up my guitar. I have been busy all day writing a new song. When the words start to come, I can only write them down. I don't have complete control over what comes out. It's as if the music possesses me, as the island does. I have already given the song a title-The Hammer.

I pulled back the hammer, my momma didn't cry
Daddy's in the slammer, I let that bullet fly
It's hard to be good, when the devil has your soul
And momma's turned your heart, into a chunk of coal

It isn't one of my typical songs; I usually sing about the ocean or love or pretty women. Most songs have all three. For some reason though, the words coming out today were dark, I hope it's not a bad omen.

I looked up again at the ship.

Where in the world is he going? There is nothing out here in this direction, other than my island. The only boats I am used to seeing out here are tourist or reporters wanting to take pictures of my island and me. The ship was now only about five hundred yards away and coming straight at me. Surely, he'll drop the wind and tack away from me any time now. I don't think the ship could possibly stop in time if it kept coming in this direction.

Not wanting to believe it could be coming straight for me; I un-wrapped a piece of pepper jack cheese and folded it onto one of my burgers. It started to melt immediately. I nervously looked back at the ship and then away quickly, as if it wouldn't keep coming if I didn't watch it.

I turned to the bar and picked out a bottle of Shiraz. I've acquired a taste for wine in the last two years mainly due to my first love, Rose.

I snuck another peak in the direction of the ship.

One hundred yards and full sails. I could now see the Captain at the helm. He had on a pirate's hat, similar to what you would see in an old movie, where the swashbucklers waved their swords and carried their knives in their teeth as they swung around the ship in combat. Sitting on the front of the ship was a woman on what looked like a teak throne. She had her feet propped up on a brass foot bar. In her hand was a rope, which was tied to the bow of the ship and she was leaning back, riding the waves, as she would a bronco. Her long blond hair was whipping in the wind and she had a big grin on her face. The waves were spraying her and she held what looked like a bottle of rum in her other hand. With her white robes flying in the wind, she looked a little haunting.

I opened the wine, put the cork to my nose, and breathed in the aroma. It was not a terribly expensive bottle of wine, but it did have a fruity hint of blackberry. My favorite. I looked again.

I was getting a little more nervous now. They were still coming straight at me. I got up and walked toward the dock. I could see the V of the bow parting the ocean, lazily rising and falling, the white water spraying into a hypnotic mist.

What the hell? At the last second I dropped my bottle of wine, which I was about to pour, and I took off running to avoid being squashed by the eighty-plus-foot schooner, which was about to inhabit my island. I looked over my shoulder and saw it bust through the docks and start digging a trench in the sand. It was still coming. Palm trees were being pushed aside, and birds were taking flight. Coconuts were falling to the ground, and palm fronds were splitting the air like arrows as they speared their way to the sand below.

The woman on the bow was still holding the rope and leaning back. She was holding the bottle of rum over her head now, her body bending to-and-fro at the waist to keep her head steady.

I ran harder, but the shadow of the great schooner was overtaking me. I felt as if I were in an old horror movie, where Godzilla was chasing me, about to pick me up with his teeth.

I tripped over a rock and fell. I landed on my guitar, which for some reason I picked up as I passed it, probably instinctually protecting it. I heard it snap. The neck was bent at a ninety-degree angle, held on only by the strings. Laying there on my back, I saw the great ship still coming at me. I closed my eyes and waited for the finale.

Then the noise stopped. I opened my eyes and saw the ship had stopped between my spread legs. Another two feet and I would have been split wide open. My family jewels would have been passed down to future generations, no more.

Chapter 1

I looked up and saw the woman on the bow, was looking straight down at me from her perch twenty feet up.

"YOU SUNNY RAY?" Her blond hair was still blowing in the wind and her robes waving around her. I thought how strange it was since there was no wind.

"Yeah," I answered, in a breathless voice.

She turned to the captain, "THIS IS HIM."

I heard the Captain let out a big, "WHOOPY," and then I heard an even louder explosion as he fired the cannon, which was mounted to the deck. The eight-inch cannon ball took out the cupola on top of my tiki hut and then blew the top off one of my giant palms.

"Sorry about that," the Lady said. "He gets a little carried away with that damn thing."

The Captain pulled a rope and the sails all collapsed to the deck, ready to be placed into their storage positions. He stood

7

on the bridge, took a deep breath, and looked around as if he had never seen land before.

"Permission to come ashore," the Captain said in a drunken slur.

"Yeah, okay, I guess," I said, trying to figure out what just happened. There is an eighty-foot schooner, fifty feet onto my island. It just came right through my dock and destroyed about ten palm trees, not to mention my tiki hut and my guitar, and for some dumb reason, I was thinking, I hope my burgers don't burn. I sneaked a glance toward them.

The captain dropped a rope ladder over the side of the ship. I could now see the name on the bow of the ship painted in big red letters, THE LADY LUCINDA. The letters were faded and weathered. They had an eerie ancient look to them.

"Lucy, give me a hand here," he ordered her, but she just waved her hand at him in a dismissing manner.

He stepped over the side, put one pirate-booted foot on the rope ladder and then threw the other leg over. He made it down about three feet before his leg slipped through the rungs and he fell, catching himself upside down. He was now hanging there, threatening to fall. I jumped up and ran to the ladder. I climbed half way up and held his shoulders so he could get his leg out.

"Fuckin' ladder," he said through gritted teeth, "I need to get a new one."

"Just let the son of a bitch fall," Lucy yelled. "He knows better than to drive up on someone's island."

I managed to help him the rest of the way down. When we were safely on the ground, he yelled at Lucy to come down.

She took off her robes, tossed them on the deck, and came over the side and down the ladder as if it was something she did every day.

8

Once on the ground I could see she was a very gorgeous, sixty something year old, girl. Her complexion was flawless. Her eyes were an unnatural shade of green-blue. Jade-like in aspect, reminding me of the jewels I once saw in an exhibition.

"Sunny Ray, I'm Louie-Louie, very nice to finally meet you," he slurred.

"Nice to meet you too," I said in a stunned voice, not knowing why I even said that. It was not nice to meet him. In fact, it was one of the most horrible first encounters, I had ever had. He almost killed me with that damn schooner. What the hell was he up to?

"Excuse me for a minute," I said, and walked to the grill and took the burgers off and placed them on a plate, which was waiting on the table next to the grill. I don't know why I was so concerned about these damn burgers. Maybe because, I still didn't want to face what just happened.

"God damn it Louie, tell him you're sorry for tearing up his island first, and then you can get down to business," Lucy said. "He has supper ready and he wants to get to it."

"I am so sorry for the damage I have done to your island paradise," he said, as proper as he could manage.

"Who are you and what do you want with me?"

"I told you, I am Louie-Louie. I have come here in desperation, to ask for your help."

Louie was looking at me but I don't think I was in focus. His hat was still askew, from the fall down the latter, and he had a faraway look in his eyes. He had long brownish grey hair, which was tied into a ponytail, with a yellow ribbon about an inch from the end. The ribbon instantly reminded me of Wild Irish Rose, my ex-girlfriend.

"Wanta Mea sent me here to ask …."

Then Louie fell forward and landed face down in the sand. He didn't move. Neither did I. He just crashed my whole world with one name–Wanta Mea.

Wanta Mea was, well, hard to explain. She was a friend, a very close friend, who I met on the island of Rumora, a few years ago.

Rumora was actually in a different dimension, a parallel universe so to speak. I took refuge there when a drug lord was chasing me from Nashville. Some friends of mine, John and his son Curt James, who had visited the island before, took me there to protect me.

There was a ritual which needed to be performed to be allowed on the island and then only if they wanted you there. The island natives worshiped rum and music. They knew of me long before I arrived, since I was a musician, but Wanta Mea, also knew me from my childhood.

She was visiting our world and happened upon me just as I was about to drown in a raging creek. She pulled me out and then she kissed me and ran away. We were only ten years old, but we were both in love for the rest of our lives. I never got the scent of honeysuckle out of my mind after that encounter. She smelled of the fragrant flower. We didn't meet again until I was twenty-two. I owe her my life, and I would do anything to help her. I love her deeply.

My island was copied after theirs. Rum City Bar was the name of my bar, as was theirs. Wanta Mea was one of the council, which ruled the island.

On my first visit to Rumora, I fell in love with the people. The island was everything I could imagine I would ever want in a world. The flowers were large and colorful and palm trees were several hundred feet tall. The island was bathed in music. The rum made you feel as if you could accomplish anything you set your mind to, and you could.

Wanta Mea was assigned to me while I was on the island. I later found out, she was the one who did the assigning. Then one day she told me she was the one who pulled me from the creek and kissed me. I visited the island as often as I could for the first year. Then after we spent time together, I fell in love with Wanta Mea again, and spent five years with her on her island. That only equaled one day in our world.

"What–how do you know Wanta Mea?" I asked, but it was no use, he was out cold.

Lucy walked over to us and looked down at him, "Stupid fuck," she spat.

"What does he mean, Wanta Mea sent him?" I asked.

Lucy stuck out her hand to shake mine. "I'm Lucy Lewis," she said.

Now that we were closer, I could see she didn't have any lines in her face. She must be a lot younger than I had first thought. She was very attractive. Her hand was soft in my grip and I could feel a tingling sensation running up my arm. Louie, on the other hand, looked to be about seventy-five or eighty, but he was quite spry for his age. Even drunk, he almost made it down the ladder.

"You'll have to excuse Louie; he won't drink much of the rum from the island, so he's not ageing too well."

"You know about the rum from the island?" I asked her. I thought myself and about six others were the only ones who knew of the rum.

There was blue rum, which kept you young and red rum, which gave you soul and green rum that made you creative. Rumora was the only place in the world, if it was actually in this world, I still don't know how that works, where you can find these rums.

"Sunny, I was drinking that rum when you were shitin' in your diapers."

11

Lucy was very colorful, if nothing else, but I had a bad feeling she was something else.

"Tell me about Wanta Mea," I said, starting to raise my voice. Nothing else in the world mattered to me at that moment.

"Rumora is in trouble Sunny. Wanta Mea asked us if we would try to find you and ask you to help them. She told us where you were, but she couldn't come herself. If she leaves, even for a minute, they might lose their advantage, and their island."

"Of course I'll help. What kind of trouble are Rumora and Wanta Mea in?"

"Let's get Louie up and put him to bed, then I'll tell you all about it, over a nice glass of blue rum."

I threw Louie over my shoulder in a fireman's carry, carried him to my apartment and laid him on the sofa. The bedroom was upstairs and I wasn't about to carry him up there. He wasn't a heavy man thank goodness, just awkward.

Lucy tucked him in while I got some glasses and poured us some rum from Lucy's bottle.

"Is this really rum from the island?" I asked her. I knew they weren't allowed to take any of the rum from the island.

"No, but I like to put a little die in my rum, so I can act like I'm there. I miss that island when I'm gone."

"Yeah, me too," I said, already getting anxious to return, even if it was for bad reasons.

Lucy looked around the room taking in all the recording equipment and the gold records on the walls. There were pictures of me with all the well-known musicians of the day and one with the president. The furniture was all island style chosen and paid for by Rose.

"You sure get around a lot," Lucy said.

"Yes, I have my share of adventure," I said, looking back at Louie.

"Louie, his real name is Louis Lewis, he likes to be called Louie-Louie, won't drink the rum on the island. He says he is strong and wise enough the way he is. Of course, that's bullshit, as you can see. But I slip him enough of it to keep him from looking any worse than he does now."

"Tell me about Rumora. Is Wanta Mea O.K.? I'll do anything I can to help them. Just tell me what to do."

"She's fine right now, but the island could be in some real trouble."

"What trouble?"

"Well, I don't know where to start. It seems, the people on the island don't laugh and sing, like they used to. They say they don't feel like it. I know it doesn't sound serious, unless you know them, and I know you do."

I thought back to when I was on the island. It was a constant party. The most jovial people you have ever seen. They played music and danced every day, all day. There were times when we played music and danced for two or three days without stopping. Drinking only rum and eating food, which would make the best New York restaurants seem like McDonalds.

"Yes, I do know the people," I said thoughtfully.

"Wanta Mea said, since you were from the outside, you might be able to figure something out if you came to visit them."

Lucy finished her rum and poured another. She didn't seem to be inebriated. I figure she can probably hold her own when it comes to drinking and anything else.

"Sunny, they're changing. They cannot survive without music and they don't seem to care. They are becoming bitter," she said, and drank down half her glass. Her blond hair blew

13

in the wind again, except there was no wind in my living room.

"I'll be glad to go back to Rumora and help them get their old life back. They are too good to let die."

"Good, we'll set sail in the morning."

"How are we going to get your schooner off the island?"

"We'll back it up," she laughed.

Chapter 2

I showed Lucy upstairs to the master bedroom and then went back out to the bar. I couldn't believe the sight. The island looked as if a hurricane had hit it. Trees were down, my cupola was lying on the ground, and there was an eighty-foot schooner on my beach.

The paint was pealing on it now. The shrouds, which covered the sails, were torn and dingy and the name, THE LADY LUCINDA, on the side was barely visible. I hadn't noticed that earlier. With the stars and dark sky for a backdrop, the ship looked very eerie.

I walked over to where my guitar was laying and picked it up. My good Taylor was broke in half. I noticed my hamburgers sitting on the table, picked one up and took a bite. It wasn't very warm, but tasted pretty good. The aroma of the burger took my senses back to a few hours ago when I first put them on the grill. My plan was to smoke a joint, play my guitar, and maybe be inspired to write another, hopefully great, song. This wasn't the way I had this evening planned at all. I walked behind the bar to fix a drink. I had to step over the broken bottle of Shiraz, which I had been planning to drink before I was interrupted. I chose a Cabernet Sauvignon and poured a full glass. I finished my burger and wine and poured another.

I walked around the ship, which was almost completely on the island, and wondered how we were ever going to get it out of here. I looked up again at the name, THE LADY LUCINDA. Anything but, I thought.

The ship looked weathered but defiantly seaworthy. They don't make them like this anymore. I thought about it being on Rumora and had to reach out and touch it just to feel like I was on the island again.

It brought back old memories. I thought I could pick up a scent of honeysuckle coming off the old wood.

I swirled the wine around my glass watching it coat the sides and then slowly sliding back down into the deep red pool. I took another sip. The wine had taken on the slight scent of honeysuckle, as if it were trying to join forces with the ship and draw me into the world of Rumora. It worked.

I walked to the rope ladder and gave it a yank, testing its strength. It seemed sound to me. I sat the glass of wine down twisting it into the sand so it wouldn't tip over before I returned. I began my accent up the ladder.

I could see how Louie could fall off this thing. It wasn't easy to keep from turning around and bouncing back first off the ship. The rope was frayed in spots to the point I didn't think it would hold me. I could hear it creaking and once it seemed to drop an inch or two.

I reached the railing and wrapped my hand around it. It was rough like it had sat in the salty weather for many years without polishing.

I threw my leg over and stepped onto the deck. It was worn and weathered as well. The ship looked to be in a lot better condition when they first arrived. It was aging before my eyes.

The smell of honeysuckle was greatly pronounced up here. I closed my eyes and took a deep breath. In my mind's eye, I could see Wanta Mea standing in front of me. Her long black hair was gently waving in the breeze, which was ever-present on Rumora. She reached out, took my hand and smiling she pulled me to her and kissed me softly on the lips.

"Help us Sunny, Please," I heard her say.

"I will. I'll be there soon," I replied.

I opened my eyes and she was gone. I felt sad now.

I walked around the ship and peered into the cabins and the bridge. The boat didn't look seaworthy anymore. There were no belongings on board. No sign anyone had been on the ship for a long time. Then there was a blast from the foghorn. I jumped.

"Sunny run. Get off the ship now!" I heard Wanta Mea say.

I knew that I had better do as she said, and try to figure out why later. I ran to the rope ladder and threw my leg over. As I was getting a good foothold, I looked back and saw three huge men coming toward me. They were semi-transparent and dressed like the men on Rumora. Cargo shorts and no shirts, but I could tell they were different. They had evil in their eyes.

I half climbed and half slid down the rope ladder and hit the ground hard. I laid there for a moment listening for signs of the men from above. Nothing.

My wine was still standing in the sand, where I had left it. I picked it up and downed it. When I got to my feet, a hand startled me, squeezing my shoulder. I turned quickly to see Lucy standing there.

"I'm sorry I didn't mean to scare you," she said in a soothing voice. "I've been watching you sitting in the sand. You looked like you were having a bad dream."

"I was on the boat," I said. "I saw three men coming after me."

"No, you didn't get on the boat. You were dreaming," she said. "The night can play tricks on your mind."

"I need to get to Rumora. Wanta Mea needs me."

"We'll get you there tomorrow. I think you should go to bed now. You'll need your rest."

"Yeah, your right."

We went back to the cabin. Louie was sound asleep and snoring quite loudly. He looked like he had a hard life. Alcohol and women were written all over his face. I wondered if I would look like that someday at the rate I was going.

"Goodnight Sunny. Big day tomorrow," Lucy said as she climbed the stairs to the bedroom.

"Goodnight Lucy," I said.

I went to the bathroom to throw some water on my face. I looked in the mirror. I had lipstick on my face. The same shade Wanta Mea wears.

Chapter 3

I decided tomorrow would be a big day indeed and I had better get some sleep, and then I remembered Lori. Lori is my girlfriend. She is also a country singer who has been very successful and she was on tour with me the last couple of months. She was coming to the island to relax with me and should be here tomorrow. I thought I better call her and give her a heads up, just in case she would rather relax somewhere else.

"Hi Lori, it's me," I said, as if she didn't know.

"Hey Sunny, can't wait to see you tomorrow."

"Yeah, about that," I said, and told her about Rumora. She knew them as well as I did. She also spent some time there with me. She was totally fixated with the island. I think she would live there the rest of her life.

"Oh, that's terrible. Do you think you can help them?"

"I don't know but I'm going to try. I thought I would call John and Curt to see if they would go with me."

John and his son Curt are the ones who introduced me to the island first. We were all being chased by drug dealers, who

19

would just as soon see us dead. It was all an unfortunate calamity, which landed us right in the middle of a drug war.

John and Curt had been to the island before. They knew no one could ever find us there, since it was in a different dimension.

John had stumbled upon the island when his boat was lost in a storm. Just when he was thinking his life was over, they rescued him and took him to the island, knowing his son Curt was a musician. Otherwise, they might have rescued him anyway, but would not have taken him to their island.

"You know they will. They love those people as much as you do. Between the three of you, I know you can help them," she said, sounding optimistic. "And I would like to go with you. I might be of some help."

"No. not this time, but thanks for the confidence. I hope your right. You can go there with me when this is over. So, what about tomorrow? You're still welcome to stay on the island," I told her, hoping she would still come.

"I'll be there. I want to be there when you return."

"Good, I'll see you then. I love you."

"Love you too," Lori said, still wishing she could return to Rumora.

I woke early the next morning, but not early enough to see how they got the ship off the island, but it was gone.

My palm trees were standing again, my cupola was back on the tiki hut, and everything seemed normal. I sat down on a bar stool and thought about what happened. Were they really here, or did I just dream all that. Then I noticed my guitar, the neck back on it, was leaning against the bar, it had a note on it.

Sunny
 We couldn't wait for you. See you there.
 Captain Louie-Louie and Lucy
Well, that confirmed my worst fears, they were here.

I walked around the beach and dock, but there was no sign that they had ever been here. I couldn't keep from laughing now, when I thought how Louie fell down the ladder and Lucy cursed him. Their marriage must be very exciting.

Chapter 4

I spent some time trying to reason what had happened. If they were really here, why didn't they take me with them?

Who were the men on the boat? Where were they from and what would they have done if they had caught me?

Why did I have lipstick on my face?

What the hell was up with Louie-Louie?

I looked at the note again. Damn, it was still here. I was hoping it was gone and this was all just a bad trip.

But, I wasn't tripping and this wasn't a dream. They were here.

Now what should I do? I know John would take me to Rumora. He and Curt would back me on anything I did. Even more, they would insist on helping the people on Rumora.

I decided I was going to have to take some kind of action.

John answered on the third ring. I filled him in on what had taken place the night before.

"You mean they were just gone, and everything was normal again?" he said, with astonishment in his voice.

"That's pretty much it. If it weren't for the note on my guitar, I would have thought I dreamed it."

"Are we going?" John asked.

"I am," I said. "You're welcome to join me if you wish."

"Let's do it. I'm due for a good fight."

"Thanks."

"Come on over, I'll be getting the boat ready," John said.

"What about Curt, do you think he'll wanna go?"

"Yeah, I think he will, but he's in Alaska with Bonnie, visiting some friends. I'll call him and let him know what's going on and let him decide."

"Okay, I'll see you in a while," I said, and hung up.

I gathered a few things I thought I might need and packed them on my forty-foot cruiser, which we use to transport guests to the island.

The boat had a warm feeling. Lori and I have made this boat our home a few romantic nights.

I turned the key and the twin 454's came to life. I drew in the lines and aimed for Marathon Key.

The morning was still and the waters calm. It was hard to believe the people I loved the most were in so much danger.

The ocean was a beautiful turquoise this morning, as it is most mornings. I passed small islands with scattered fishing boats around them. The seven-mile bridge had its share of small fishing boats too. I thought about how life went on and most people are oblivious to anything that doesn't directly affect their world. I pulled into Johns dock forty-five minutes later.

Rose, his wife, met me at the dock. The two of us had history. She was the first girl I was ever really in love with. She hugged and kissed me. I still cherish every second I spend with her, even though she is very happily married to my best friend. She was dressed in short shorts and a bikini top, which did little to cover her voluptuous breasts.

Rose and I met in Evansville, Indiana, where I was born and raised. It was my seventeenth birthday and my friends took me to "The Landing Strip Club," a strip club by the airport. There I met Rose, "Wild Irish Rose" when she came to the stage.

Her red hair looked as though it was on fire as she twirled around the stage.

We ended up lovers, in an affair that lasted for four months. Rose finally wised up and left Evansville and me in the dust. It was a good move on her part. She was five years older than I was, but I lied to her about my age. Something she later discovered. She was my first and I'll never forget her. I couldn't believe it when I found her again down here in Marathon, when I met John.

"Hi Rose, good to see you," I choked out.

"You too Sunny; I can't believe Rumora is in trouble."

"I'm afraid they might be."

I noticed a fuel truck backing down the lane next to the house. He was heading to Johns seventy-five foot Offshore cruiser. It would be topped off, for our journey to Rumora.

Rose walked me to the house holding my hand. The palm trees lining the walk created a shaded canopy for us to walk through. The flowers added a beauty to the landscape that paralleled any picture you might find in those home and garden magazines. I knew Rose did all the garden work herself. It was her therapy.

24

The house was a Florida style mansion. It towered over us as we entered through the open wall from the patio. The interior was even more impressive than the exterior. The woodwork was hand carved and the stair balusters were forged iron. The furnishings probably cost more than my entire island and bar. Rose has done very well for herself.

"Sit down and I'll get you some tea," Rose said. "John will be down in a minute."

"Thanks. I'm a little parched from the boat trip, but if you don't mind, I would rather have a scotch."

She looked at me for a second and said, "You must be very worried. I've never seen you drink before lunch."

"I am."

Rose brought the scotch and sat with me for a few minutes while we waited for John to come down. I couldn't resist sneaking a peak at her legs and breasts when she wasn't looking, but she caught me.

"Some things never change, do they?" she said, with a tilt of her head and a little grin.

"It's not my fault. I was born that way."

John came down the steps.

John James was fifty-six years old, but looked to be only about forty-five. The rum from Rumora has kept him young. He visits the island about twice a year.

"Sorry Sunny, I was talking to Curt. He's going to join us on the island tomorrow. He'll fly his seaplane out there. I'll tell Paris to be on the lookout for him."

Paris is the keeper of the dock on Rumora. He decides who comes to the island and who does not. He's six foot ten inches of solid muscle and one of the most jovial guys I have ever met.

"Sunny, did you say the name on the schooner was, The Lady Lucinda?" John asked.

"Yeah, have you heard of it?"

"I don't know, but it sound's familiar. Let me check something."

John walked to the bookshelf, pulled out a copy of "Greatest American Yachts" and thumbed through the pages.

"Here it is. The Lady Lucinda was lost at sea during a hurricane in 1926. Captain Louis Lewis and his wife Lucinda were considered, lost at sea. Captain Lewis was an avid guitar player and Lucinda was a jazz singer. They met through their music and married six weeks later."

"Wow, I guess they were saved by the people on Rumora and decided to live there," Rose said.

"I guess so. They're good people. I'm glad they were saved," I said thoughtfully.

John put the book back on the shelf and turned to me. "You never know who you are going to see on Rumora."

"I know. It's scary sometimes."

"The boat will be ready in about an hour. Are you hungry?" John asked.

"Yeah I am a little hungry. You wanna go to Porky's and get a bite?"

"Sounds good to me," John said.

"Me too," Rose said.

"I'll drive," I said, "I wanna get Bloodshot out and stretch his legs."

Bloodshot is my fifty-four Chevy truck. We've been through a lot together and I like to drive him whenever I can. I rebuilt him in Evansville and John had him painted for me down here. It was a great surprise.

"Good," Rose said, "I love to ride in that old truck."

Bloodshot was parked in John's garage. He kept him here for me while I was on tour.

The smell of the leather interior brought back memories. Rose got in on Johns side, slid over and John rode shotgun. Her leg was against mine and I could feel a shiver run through my body. I know I shouldn't feel this way, but they say you never get over your first love. I would never follow up on any of my feelings, but I still have them.

I turned the key, pushed the starter button and Bloodshot came to life. The three twenty-seven cubic inch engine had a deep-throated roar that just sounded fast.

We pulled out of the driveway and turned toward Sombrero beach. It was only a block away. I was talking to John when Rose shouted, "LOOK OUT." I slammed on the brakes instinctively. When I looked up there was a man standing in the road in front of us. He had on cargo shorts and no shirt. The part, which chilled us to the bone, was that he was at least six foot ten inches tall and had a golden complexion and black hair down to his waist, just like the men from Rumora.

He stared at us for a few seconds and then held up one long finger and pointed and shook his head from side to side, as if to tell us no. Then he just vanished.

"Son of a bitch," Rose said.

"What the hell was that," John muttered in a tone that indicated he might not have seen what he thought he saw.

"I believe that was a warning," I said. "He had to be from Rumora."

We sat in the middle of the street for at least a full minute and then we looked at each other. Rose was white. John and I both had our mouths open in disbelief.

I took my foot off the brake, stepped on the gas, drove Bloodshot to the end of the street, and turned left toward Porky's.

Chapter 5

We looked at the people surrounding us. They were getting chairs and coolers out of their trunks and herding their children across the lot toward the beach. No one seemed to have noticed the event, which had just taken place.

"Did we really see that?" I asked them.

"Yeah, I think we did."

"Son of a bitch," Rose said.

I looked at her for a second and then started laughing. I don't know why I thought it was so funny, but I did. They started laughing too and then we all just stopped.

"This isn't funny. Someone's trying to tell us something," I said.

"I think your right," John said. "What do you think the message was?"

"I think he was trying to tell us to leave it alone."

"Me too, but that's not gonna happen."

"We might be in for some rough times when we get to Rumora," I said, and then looking at Rose; "We'll be okay though, they would never hurt anyone," I told her, trying to comfort her.

"You don't know that. You don't know what has happened to them now," she said in a panicked voice.

"Don't worry Rose, we'll be careful," John said, trying to ease her concern. "I'm sure he was just trying to tell us to be careful."

"I'm sure he was," Rose said angrily.

We drove on for a few minutes without saying anything, but I could tell Rose wasn't going to drop this.

"I don't think you two should go," she finally said.

"Rose, you know we have to," John said, his tone relaying a note of finality, so Rose would know there was no further discussion needed on this topic.

"Well, I don't like it," she said, and that was the end of that.

We pulled into Porkey's parking lot and turned off the engine. Rose hugged John, kissed him and then did the same to me. She didn't say anything and neither did we.

Porkey's was our favorite restaurant. We have spent numerous nights here with all our friends. One of our friends, Fast Freddie plays guitar and sings here a few nights a week. The ceiling and the one wall, there is only one the rest of the area is open to the docks and stage, are decorated with signs, dollar bills, flags, and names. Guests write their words of wisdom on all available spaces.

We had a glass of wine, ordered some jerked chicken, and made small talk. We were still in a daze from earlier, and were trying to skirt the topic.

When the chicken came, we picked at it but no one really felt like eating. We finally paid our bill and left. Just as we were getting in Bloodshot, we saw the man from earlier, standing in the parking lot again.

John got out and walked toward him. The man retreated a few steps and then stopped. We could see John talking with him. The visitor held up his hand as if in a half salute and so did John, then the man vanished once more. John turned and walked back to the truck.

"What was that all about," Rose asked him when he got in.

"It seems there really is something wrong on Rumora and this guy says if we go there we could be in real danger. He said the people aren't as friendly as they used to be and he wanted to warn us, because they still don't want any outsiders hurt on their island."

"Did he say what the problem was?" I asked.

"He just said the people and the island have changed."

"John, I don't think you should go. I don't have any choice. You know I love Wanta Mea and I have to go. I'll come back as soon as I can get some answers," I said.

"Look Sunny, I'm the one who took you to Rumora in the first place. I've been going there ever since they saved me from the hurricane I was stuck in years ago. If it weren't for them, I would be dead already. I owe them, and I'm going with you."

Rose started to cry. We both looked at her, our hearts breaking. I have never seen her cry and it hurt. John held her and I patted her on the leg and told her we would be okay.

"Please be careful," she said. "I love both of you and I can't stand the thought of losing either one of you.

WE drove back to the house and arrived just as the fuel truck was leaving.

"I guess we'll just load the boat and we're ready to go," John said.

"I'll get my bags out of my boat and meet you there," I told John, to let he and Rose have some time together.

I was waiting on the boat when John and Rose came back out. John was carrying his bag and Rose had a grocery sack.

"I made you guys some sandwiches for the trip," she said, her tears now dried up and her eyes green again.

"Thank you," I said, and reached for the bag.

Rose took my hand, pulled me close to her, and kissed me. "You take care of yourself and don't let anything happen to John."

"Don't worry, we'll be fine," I told her with a smile. "You take care of Bloodshot, and if you want to drive him it's okay."

Rose had a Bentley GT Speed in her garage, so I don't think she'll be driving Bloodshot, but it did get a smile from her and that was what I was aiming for.

Chapter 6

John maneuvered the yacht out of the canal and into the open sea. Our journey to Rumora promised to be a pleasant one. The temperature was seventy-eight degrees and the wind was at six knots.

As the skies started to darken, we could see the stars beginning to appear. We would need the stars to help us navigate to Rumora. In the distance, I could see a few black clouds and hint of pink peeking through the gap in their formation. A distant thunderstorm that would never reach us. By the time it arrived, we would be in another dimension. In the second dimension, the weather was always perfect. If they want rain, they will conjure it up.

A few minutes later, we stopped the boat and John got the sextant out of its case, to navigate the stars.

He taught me how to read the stars, so I could navigate at night if I was ever out here and I lost my GPS system. Tonight he read the stars and told me which way to steer. After a series of left and right turns, we stopped the boat and started to prepare for our final step into the second dimension of Rumora.

We stowed our gear to protect it from the heavy fog we knew was to come and threw a line over the bow for Paris to tow us to the island. With that finished, we went below to wait.

A half hour passed and we were still waiting.

"Do you think Paris is gonna come for us?" I asked John.

"He'll be here. I think he's giving it some thought though."

Another fifteen minutes passed before we felt the bump on the side of the boat.

"There he is," I said. "I was starting to worry."

We felt the boat rotate and start to pick up speed. Paris was towing us to Rumora by swimming and pulling us with the rope, which we had dropped over the bow.

The boat finally bumped the dock and we went topside.

Paris was standing on the dock as always, but this time he did not greet us with his usual candor. He just stared at us.

We were in the second dimension.

Chapter 7

"Hello Paris," John said, breaking the silence.
"Hello John, Hello Sunny, welcome to Rumora."
"Thank you Paris. We heard you might need some help. That's why we came."
"Yes, it does appear we need help. Our island is not the way it was. The people, including myself, aren't happy like we were."
"Do you know why?" John asked.
"No, but it is so. I accept it."
I noticed the island was still. There was usually a lot going on for a non-touristy island. The music was always playing and you could hear the islanders laughing and singing from the docks.
"I don't hear any music playing. This is the first time I've come here and not heard music," I said.

"No one really wants to listen to it. It just sounds like noise."

"Don't worry Paris, we're going to help. We'll find out what the problem is," I said.

Paris just looked down at the dock and said, "I hope so." His six foot ten inch frame looked small now. He was a beaten man.

We gathered our bags and walked with Paris to the bar. The trail, which was usually lined with exquisite flowers and singing birds, looked barren. The feel of the whole island was different. The path, which would normally be raked in a decorative pattern, was full of footprints and dead leaves.

The sign over the bar which reads, "RUM CITY BAR" was not lit. There was no one at the bar, which is usually packed. The wooden bar stools sat empty. The thatched tiki hut looked as if it were just abandoned and left to rot in the jungle. The band stand had several guitars lying on the floor, as if they were just dropped haphazardly by the musicians, who chose not to return.

I walked up on the stage, which I've played on many times with big stars such as Billie Jay Player and John Denver, but that is another story, and picked up a guitar. It buzzed. It was still plugged into the amp and left on.

I started playing Rum City Bar, the song I wrote for them one time when I was here.

To my surprise and delight, people started coming out of the jungle and gathering around the stage. Before long, some were dancing and everyone was smiling again.

Wanta Mea worked her way to the front of the crowd and yelled at me, "SUNNY, THANK YOU."

I finished the song and everyone cheered. I laid down the guitar and went to Wanta Mea. She put her arms around me and kissed me long and hard on the lips.

She was as stunning as I remember; six foot two inches tall, golden tan, with dark black hair down to her waist. She wore cargo shorts as she usually does and her breasts were only covered by a lei.

"Wanta Mea, good to see you again."

"Good to see you too, Sunny. Thank you so much for the music. When we play, it does not sound good anymore."

"We'll figure it out," I said.

Then Youramine and John joined us. Youramine is another native of Rumora. She is about six foot three with skin tone a little lighter than Wanta Mea's, and has blond hair down to her waist, another real knock out. She was very helpful when we were battling the drug lords a few years ago.

"Hello Youramine," I said.

She walked to me and kissed me, and Wanta Mea kissed John. I love the way they greet you on this island.

"Thank you Sunny. That was very beautiful. It was good to hear music again. Everyone is happy," Youramine said excitedly.

"Would you like some rum?" Wanta Mea asked.

"No thanks, not right now. I think I'd like to keep my head clear while I think about this."

"Okay, we will take you to your cabin so you can shower and get ready for the concert tonight," Youramine said.

"Oh, is there a concert tonight?"

"Yes, there is now. You will play for us, please," she begged.

"Okay, I'll be glad to."

"YEAH!" Wanta Mea yelled.

They took us to our cabins, which were about a hundred yards from the bar. The path to the cabin was lush and green. I could hear the birds singing and the flowers were actually growing before our eyes.

"This is wonderful. See what just one song can do," Wanta Mea said.

Once inside I knew what would happen. Wanta Mea would enter the shower with me and wash me all over. It was something we have always done and she loved doing it as much as I did.

The cabin was built of wood and had a thatched roof. The front porch had some rocking chairs on it and there were flower boxes on the windows with colorful flowers growing in them.

We entered the cabin and I tossed my bag on the bed. The room was decorated in an island fare. Colorful tables and chairs, none of which matched, but that was the theme they were going for. On the walls were pictures of John and Rose, Curt and Bonnie and Lori and I.

There were exact duplicates of my gold and platinum records and also Lori's.

The cabin was designed and decorated differently, every time I came. If I came alone, there was only one cabin. If two of us came, there were two and so on.

"Are you ready for a shower?" I asked her.

"Sunny, you know I have always loved you, but I have to tell you something."

I didn't like this. A line, which started like that, almost never ended well.

"You can tell me anything, Wanta Mea."

"When I was a teenager, I had a boyfriend here on the island. We were supposed to get married, but he got into a fight with another man. That is strictly forbidden on Rumora. He was exiled from the island for ten years. He returned last month. We are seeing each other again. I don't know if we will marry, but I need to give it a chance. I promised him I would when he left. His name is Tahoe."

I felt like someone hit me in the gut. One of the givens of my life was that Wanta Mea would always love me and I would always love her.

"I understand Wanta Mea. I hope whatever you do, is what will make you happy."

"It would make me happy to spend the rest of my life with you, but I must keep my promise to try."

"I know you do. Will I see you at the bar tonight?" I asked.

"Yes, we will be there."

"Good, I'll see you then."

She turned and left and my heart sank. I never even thought of the possibility of losing her. The last time I was here, I brought Lori with me. Our upcoming schedules will keep us from each other for a while, and now Wanta Mea is gone too. Things are defiantly going downhill.

Chapter 8

I took my shower and thought about the many times Wanta Mea shared this with me. I would miss her, but I can't stand in the way of what she thinks is right.

When I got out of the shower, I wrapped my towel around me and went to the kitchen to get a glass of rum. I was surprised by Louie-Louie and Lucy standing in my living room.

"Well, I see you made it," Louie said.

"I told you he would be here," Lucy said. "He's a good man, and he cares about these people."

"It's good to see you two again," I said.

"Have you figured out the problem yet? Why doesn't the music play?" Louie asked in a slight slur. "And why is everyone so grumpy?"

"Damn it Louie, he just got here, it will take him a few minutes to figure this all out," Lucy said, smacking Louie on the back of the head.

"I think it might take me more than a few minutes. I don't even know where to start," I said, trying to defend myself.

"Start from the beginning," Lucy said.

"The beginning of what?"

"The beginning of the Island. Find out what gave the Island its power in the first place, and then maybe you can figure out what went wrong," Lucy said.

"Yeah, that's what I'd do. That ought to make it easy. Just start from the beginning," Louie said.

I could see this wasn't going to be easy. These two, I think, might have had too much rum over the years. How do they think I'm going find out, the secrete of the island?

"Do you two have any idea how the island got its power?" I asked.

"Shit, how do you think we would know," Louie said.

"You have to ask the island, not us," Lucy said.

"Ask the island?" I said. "Where is the islands ear? I'll just go whisper in it."

"Don't get all sarcastic with us now. We're just making suggestions," Lucy said.

"Yeah, do a little investigating. The answers aren't just going to come to you," Louie said, still slurring his words.

"Okay," I said, giving up, "I promise I'll do what I can to find out what the problem is."

They said they would be glad to help me if I needed anything. With that, they turned to leave. Louie stopped.

"Hey, is that your guitar?" he said, looking at the Taylor propped against the wall.

"It's the one they keep here for me to play while I'm on the island."

"Mind if I give it a try?"

"Not at all," I said, wondering how he was going to manage to play in the shape he was in.

Louie picked up the guitar and started to play. I was amazed at the sound he could get out of that guitar. It sounded like two or three guitars playing.

He played an old jazzy song, which I recognized but couldn't name.

"Thanks," he said when he finished, and propped the guitar back against the wall.

"Show off," Lucy said. "He used to play a lot, but I think this is the first time I've heard him in fifty years," she said to me. "You still got it," she said to Louie, and hugged him.

That reminded me of something I had been wondering about.

"Do you know where John Denver and Amelia Earhart are? And has Billy Jay Player been here recently?"

"John and Amelia still live on the other side of the island. No one ever goes there, they respect their privacy. There are other famous people there too. We haven't seen Billy Jay for about six weeks."

"Okay, thanks."

They said goodbye and left.

I thought about the first time I saw John Denver sing at Rum City Bar. That was quite a shock. Wanta Mea told me they pulled him from his airplane before it crashed, but left his body. I didn't pretend to understand. Too deep for me.

Then I saw Amelia Earhart. They said she landed safely in the Pacific, but her plane was sinking. They took her from the plane and brought her here along with her navigator Fred. She decided she wanted to stay here forever.

I went next door and knocked on John's door. He was just getting out of the shower and Youramine answered the door naked.

This isn't the first time I've seen her naked, but I was still surprised at how lovely she was.

"Sunny, come in. John will be out in a minute."

"Thank you," I said, and stepped in trying not to stare.

John's cabin was decorated in a nautical theme and the furniture was all teak.

Youramine didn't bother to cover up. Instead, she offered me a glass of Blue Rum, which I refused. Saying I still want to keep my mind clear.

She sat down next to me on the sofa and drank her rum.

"Youramine," I said, "Do you have any idea how the island got its power in the first place? What makes the music so important that the island can't survive without it?"

"No, the Island has always had the power. Music and Rum, they are the soul and the blood. This has never happened before."

"Does anyone know?"

"Know what?" John said as he entered the room.

I filled him in on Louie and Lucy's thoughts of investigation.

"That would make sense, but how are we supposed to do that?" he asked, not really expecting an answer.

"I don't know if anyone knows," Youramine said. "That is a question we have never asked."

"I'd like to have a meeting with you and Wanta Mea tonight. Bring Paris and Reddi with you," I told Youramine.

"That will not be a problem. We will meet with you before the party."

"Youramine, we might need to be allowed into the third dimension in order to find the truth," John said.

"I will talk to the council," she said.

Youramine got up and walked to the bathroom. When she came out she was dressed in her shorts but still had no top on. She picked it up from the chair across from us and slipped it on.

"I will see you here at five o'clock," she said.

"That'll be fine," I told her.

She kissed us both. When she kissed me she whispered in my ear, "Wanta Mea still loves you."

Chapter 9

After she left, John and I decided to walk around the island and explore a bit. Maybe we could find something out of place, or some kind of clue as to what has changed the island.

It was futile. We had no clue as to what to look for. We were standing by the pond, where we swam with the girls in the past. The waterfalls still looked the same, as did everything else. It was a beautiful crystal blue pond, with a two hundred foot waterfalls, which came from a fog toped mountain. We worked our way around the pond to the falls, so we could see behind it. The spray was heavy and we could barely even see each other. I thought I saw something move in the water. When I looked down I was struck on the back of the head and I went down. The falls caught me and dragged me into the pond. I could feel it pushing me to the bottom, but I couldn't fight it, then everything went black.

I woke up lying on the rocks around the pond. John was bent down over me.

"What happened?" I asked, my head feeling like it was on fire.

"I don't know. I saw you go in the water, so I jumped in to pulled you out. You were down there for five minutes before I found you. Are you alright?"

"Yeah, I think so. My head hurts. I think someone hit me with something pretty hard."

"I didn't see anyone, but I couldn't see much of anything in all that spray."

John helped me up and we slowly found our way back to our cabins.

Other than the pain I had in the back of my head, I felt surprisingly good, for being under water for five minutes. Why didn't I drown?

There was a knock at our door. When John opened it, Wanta Mea was standing there.

"Is Sunny alright?" she asked, her eyes wide.

"He's fine. Why do you ask?"

"I had a bad feeling about him."

"Come on in and see for yourself."

Wanta Mea came in, sat down next to me and put her arms around me. She started kissing me all over my face.

"I'm okay," I told her. "You don't have to worry."

"Sunny, what happened to you?"

I told her the whole story. When I was done, I asked her why I didn't drown.

"I have told you before; nothing on this island will hurt you. Not even the island itself."

"Well, something hurt me. I could have died."

"It was not the island, but it seems we have someone that does not want you looking for answers."

"I'll have to be more careful from now on; I think your right."

"Wanta Mea," John said, "we have to find out what gave the island its strength in the first place. Do you know who would know this?"

"Maybe, but I don't know if they would talk to you."

"Who, and why wouldn't they talk to me?"

"It is the Sovereign One. It has absolute supremacy over our world. It has been here since the beginning."

"Kind of like God," I said.

"No, it answers to God."

"Can I meet with the Sovereign one?"

"Maybe, I will talk to my mother, she will know."

AT five o'clock Wanta Mea, Youramine, Reddie and Paris arrived at our cabin.

"Come on in," I said.

The three girls kissed John and me, as they entered.

Reddie was as striking as the other two, if not more so. She has always been with us when we get together, but I never knew much about her. Their other friend, Takeame, was always with Reddie, but not today.

"You didn't bring Takeame?" I asked.

"No, she is not feeling well today. I think the island is making her sick," Reddie said.

"That's too bad. I hope we can figure out what the problem is before someone gets hurt."

"We have faith in you two. We know you will help us. You have already brought music to our island and it has responded by coming alive again," Wanta Mea said.

"We'll do our best. We promise."

We sat down and John brought Rum in for all of us. I declined again, but it wasn't easy. This Rum makes you feel better than anything else I have ever experienced. Maybe tonight after the concert I would have some before I go to bed.

"Did you talk to your mother about me meeting with the Sovereign One?" I asked Wanta Mea.

"Yes," she said, and giggled.

"What so funny?"

"Why don't you ask my mother yourself?" she said, and looked at Reddie.

"I'll be glad to. When can I meet her?"

"Right now," she said. "Sunny this is my mother, Reddie, and Reddie this is Sunny," she introduced.

"You mean Reddie is your mother?" I said in astonishment.

"Yes, I'm sorry we have never told you before, but we didn't think it mattered," Reddie said.

"I guess the Rum has kept you young. I should have known that if you could live forever on the island, you couldn't age forever."

"Okay, Reddie, how do I go about meeting him?"

"First of all it isn't him. It is her."

"The Sovereign One is a girl?"

"Yes, are you surprised?"

"Well, I guess I shouldn't be; the council is all women."

"So, how do I meet her?"

"First you have to show that you are worthy to meet her."

"How do I do that?"

"You must take her the head of a fire breathing dragon."

47

Chapter 10

I could feel myself turning white and weak in the knees. The look on my face must have been comical because Wanta Mea started laughing. "Mother!" she said, "don't tell him that, he will leave the island and never come back."

"Okay, just kidding," Reddie said. "If you want to meet with her, I will arrange it."

I could feel myself relaxing a bit and I could breathe again.

"You scared me there for a minute," I said. "I was already picturing myself with a big sword fighting a dragon."

"No need for that, but still, it will not be easy to talk to her. I don't know if she has ever met with one which is not a native of the island."

"Will you try to arrange it for tomorrow?"

"I will try, but now we must go to the bar for a concert."

With that, they all stood to go.

"Paris, are you alright? You didn't say a word," I asked.

"I am just tired. I feel a little weak."

"We have to find the problem fast," John said. "I think this is taking a big toll on everyone on the island."

They all left saying they would see us in a few minutes at the bar.

John and I gathered a few items for the concert and walked the path to the bar. There was a crowd waiting for us, but they were fairly docile. They were already growing weak and tired after the earlier song. I could see the effect didn't last long.

Wanta Mea came to us with a young man. They were holding hands.

"Sunny, I would like for you to meet Tahoe," she said, turning to him and bowing slightly.

"Nice to meet you, Tahoe," I said.

"It is nice to meet you too, Sunny. I have heard a lot about you. I hope you can help us. We are not the same people we used to be and I fear for the island and its people."

"I'll do what I can."

"Thank you. I am sure your concert will help us tremendously."

I took the stage, plugged the guitar into the amp, and strummed a few cords. The music coming from the amps sounded perfect.

I made an introduction and thanked everyone for allowing me to visit their island again. Then I started playing some of my favorite songs.

The crowd was coming alive. They were singing along with me and a few of their band members joined me on the stage.

They were playing their instruments now with no problem.

Whatever the problem is, music seems to override it. As long as I play, they can play. I wondered if I stopped, how long they could play without me.

I played a few more songs and watched Wanta Mea dance with her boyfriend. He seemed to be a very nice guy. I was hoping I wouldn't like him, but I did. If they stay together, I hope she will be happy.

I saw Paris laughing and dancing too. That was a good sign. He seemed to have gotten his strength back already.

After an hour, I announced I was going to take a break. I sat at a table with John, Reddie, Youramine and Takeame, who showed up after the music had played for a few minutes. She said she was feeling better.

That was good to hear. I have grown close to all of them and I wanted them all well.

The band kept playing. They sounded great. I hoped it would last.

Wanta Mea and Tahoe joined us at the table. Tahoe held up one hand and signaled the waitress to bring a round of rum for the table.

A tray of blue rum arrived immediately. "To your youth," Tahoe said, and we all drank our rum. I could feel it go through me. It instantly relaxed the muscles and made me feel younger and stronger. The best thing about the rum—other than the obvious benefit of youth—is that you can drink all you want and never have a hangover.

I had one more rum, and then joined the band on stage again. It was truly a magical night.

I told them about our world and how it was in turmoil.

"Things just aren't as good as they used to be," I said. "We have too many enemies and can't live in peace. I wrote this song about our country. It's called, Country Ain't Country No More," then I sang it.

I got in my old truck and took myself a ride
Off across the city, into the country side
Ain't been here in about a year
And I got a big surprise

Well the cows are gone and where is that barn
That used to be on the right
Any one seen that old oak tree, I'd park under on summer
nights
The fields are bare and right over there, used to be a big
lake
Now the lake is gone and a house has spawned
I think that's a big mistake
But it all sank in when around the bend
I saw the houses and cars,
The sign said keep out neighborhood watch
It was protected by gates and bars

What ever happened to the Country
Checkin' your hat at the door
The country is changin' the worlds rearranging
And the country ain't the country no more
... ...

I finished my song and got a round of applause.

When the concert was over everyone thanked me for saving the island and shook my hand and sent rum to my table. It was a celebration.

Takeame walked me back to my cabin. That was something Wanta Mea usually did.

"Would you like for me to come in and help you with your shower?" Takeame asked.

"Not tonight Takeame. Thank you though, but I think I'll just rest and think about what I need to do tomorrow."

"That is okay. I know that your heart is sad to lose Wanta Mea. Maybe she will come back to you. I know she wants to. We also know you still love Lori too, but she is in a different world. That is okay also."

"Takeame, I love you too."

"I know you do, and I love you."

She turned and left. On an island, which was full of people who loved me, I sure felt all alone.

Chapter 11

The next morning Lori arrived at Rose's house. Lori is about five foot eight inches tall with short black hair, full breasts and an angelic face. She knows about the history between Rose and me and understands. They have become very close friends. They sat and talked about what could be happening on Rumora. No one could come up with a logical explanation.

"When will Curt and Bonnie be here?" Lori asked.

"Sometime this afternoon."

"Good, it will be nice to see them again."

Rose had made some Margaritas for Lori and herself. They were drinking and talking about old times when they heard the front door open, Curt and Bonnie came in.

"So, you got started without me, I see." Bonnie said.

Bonnie was about 5feet 10 inches tall, with black hair that hung down to the middle of her back. She was extremely beautiful, slim and had a "Hippie" look to her. She was wearing a paisley print mini skirt, alabaster see-through blouse, and leather knee boots.

She ran a boarding house for singer songwriters in Nashville. I met her when I first arrived on the scene. After meeting her, I realized we also had a mutual bond in Curt. She and Curt now run a publishing company in Nashville.

"Hey Lori, Hi mom," Curt said to the two women.

Rose was five years younger than Curt, but he likes to tease her, since she was married to his father.

"Why didn't you call for us to pick you up at the airport?" Rose said.

Curt had landed his Cesena 350 at the Marathon airport. When they were getting their bags out of the plane, Paul, a pilot friend of Curt's saw them and offered them a ride home, since he was coming down this way anyway. It was only five minutes from the airport.

"Paul gave us lift," Curt told her.

"Well sit down for a few minutes and I'll see if I can find two more Margarita's."

They had their drinks while Rose filled Curt in on the events at Rumora, as far as she knew.

She told him about the man in the street, and then later in the parking lot.

"That doesn't sound good at all," Curt said. "I'm leaving first thing in the morning. I need to get the pontoons bolted to my plane. I've never tried to find Rumora from the air, but I think they will find me if I get close enough."

"I don't like any of this. There is no telling what's going on there and being in a different dimension, anything could happen," Bonnie said.

"Yeah, your right. I'm not going to try to deny it, but I don't have a choice," Curt said.

"That's what John and Sunny said. And I know your right, but I still don't like it," Rose said, her voice shaking again. Lori took her hand.

"Don't worry about us; the girls on the island would never let anything happen to us."

"I don't think they have the power that they used to have. I think something really bad has happened there," Lori said. "Please don't go."

They sat in silence, thinking for a while, and then Curt said, "I can't stand the thought of anything happening to them, I have to go."

Curt left for the airport and busied himself getting his plane ready for the trip.

Chapter 12

Lori, Rose and Bonnie decided they would go to Sunny's island, while the men were on Rumora.

It would be private there and they would be easy to find, if the guys needed them.

Curt had the plane ready and fueled. "I'll be back before you even know I'm gone," he told Bonnie.

"Just be careful and watch over the other guys too."

"Tell Sunny, I love him," Lori said. "And say "Hi" to Wanta Mea too."

"Will do; now, you girls go to the island and enjoy yourselves."

Curt started his plane and throttled it out to the open water. He turned applying full power, skimmed across the water and lifted into the sky. He made a three sixty, tipped his wings as he flew over the girls, and then disappeared into the early morning clouds.

Curt watched his GPS until he thought he was in the vicinity of the portal they always slipped through on the yacht. He descended, skimmed the waves, and brought the plane to rest in the middle of the ocean.

This was weird. He had never just landed out here with no land in sight and he had never been here in the middle of the day. It had always been at night, using the stars to navigate. "I hope this works," he said to himself.

He stepped out of the plane, threw the rope into the water, which he had tied to the front of the plane and got back in the cockpit to wait for Paris.

Fifteen minutes later a thick fog enveloped the plane and he felt a bump. Then the plane spun around and started to move across the water. Though he couldn't see anything, because of the fog, he knew Paris was towing him to the island.

The plane stopped, lightly tapping the dock and the fog lifted. Curt looked up and saw Parris standing on the dock with a big grin on his face.

"Son Curt, welcome to Rumora."

"Hello Paris, how are you?"

"I am very good, now that Sunny has brought music back to our island."

"Glad to hear that. I was hoping he would."

Curt climbed from the plane and walked with Paris to the center of the island where the bar was located. On the way, Paris filled Curt in on a few of the events that have taken place recently on the island, including Wanta Mea's boyfriend returning and the attack on Sunny.

John and I were sitting on stools at the bar. "Curt," I yelled, "I see you made it."

"Hello son," John said, and got up and hugged him.

"Well, it looks like I'm too late to be the hero. You seem to have everything in order here."

"I don't know about that Curt," I said. "It seems that we both have hangovers this morning. That's something I've never had before on this island. I'm afraid the rum might have affected us in a bad way."

"Is anything else wrong?"

"Don't know yet. We just got up."

Curt, who was thirty five, looked around twenty five and John who was fifty eight, looked around thirty eight. The Rum from the island has managed to make them look young because they come here about three times a year and drink it while they are here.

Wanta Mea and Tahoe appeared at the bar, startling the three of them.

"Sorry, we didn't mean to scare you," Tahoe said.

I introduced Tahoe to Curt. "Nice to meet you," Curt said.

"And you too," Tahoe said. "Wanta Mea has spoken of you as well as Sunny and John. I feel like have known all of you for a long time."

Although Curt didn't want to, because of Wanta Mea, he liked Tahoe. He seemed to be a good match for her.

Wanta Mea kissed Curt and said, "Did you see all the flowers blooming on the island since Sunny brought us music? We thought they were dead."

"Yes. The island has never looked more lovely, and neither have you," Curt said.

"Thank you."

While everyone was catching up on the events, I picked up a guitar leaning against the bar and started to play a tune, which had been going through my mind.

"Woo," Curt said. "You better tune that thing."

"Your right, it sounds pretty bad."

I tried to tune the guitar but I couldn't make it sound good, no matter what I did.

"Uh-oh," I said. "This isn't good."

"Let me try," Curt said.

Curt took the guitar and started to play. It sounded just right.

"Something has affected me. Now I can't make the music play," I said.

Curt played a song and then handed the guitar to me. I played a song and it sounded good.

"It's the music again. It can override whatever is affecting us. Since Curt isn't affected yet, he can make music. His music can temporarily cure me, like mine did with the band."

Reddi appeared beside Wanta Mea, startling us again.

"Sorry," she said.

"Hi Curt," Reddi said and then kissed him.

"Reddie," I said. "Have you talked to the Sovereign One for me yet?"

"Yes, she does not like the idea of talking to you, but she does like that you are trying to help us, so she said she would talk to you for a short time."

"Well, I guess that is all I could expect. When can I see her?"

"Three days."

"Okay then. I'll do what I can in the meantime."

♫

Wanta Mea watched Sunny as he played his guitar. She felt the love stirring down deep inside her, which she has felt for him since she was ten. Even though she had an obligation to Tahoe, she didn't know if she could go through with their relationship. She felt she would be shamed. She wanted Sunny, that is, as much of him as she could have.

Why shouldn't Sunny be hers? She had as much right to be happy as anyone else. Things were not right. Not yet.

Chapter 13

Sunny, Curt and John went back to their cabins to go over what information they had gathered so far. They had the uneasy feeling that they were being watched, as they walked the trail. Once inside the cabin John walked to the window and peaked out. He thought he saw someone moving in the jungle, which bordered the cabin.

"I think we're being followed," John said.

"Yeah, I got that feeling too," I said. "Someone is uncomfortable with our presence here."

"Okay," Curt said. "So far we know someone tried to kill Sunny. Luckily, the island would not take part in drowning you. We also know that something affected Sunny's music now that he has been on the island for a while. But what?"

"First of all, why would someone want to kill me? That makes me believe that the problem with the island is manmade. If it were just something gone wrong with the island, no one would have a reason to kill me," I said.

"What about Tahoe? Maybe he's jealous," John said.

"Yeah, I thought about that, but he doesn't seem the type. He seems to be happy to be back and has the good of the island at heart."

"I wonder where he was for the last ten years." Curt said.

"I don't know, but I think that's something I should ask Wanta Mea."

"Let's explore the island again," John said. "Maybe we overlooked something. The last time we were rather rudely interrupted."

We set out on a mission to find anything that didn't seem normal. That was a tough job since we were in a different dimension and everything on the island was abnormal to us.

Youramine saw us heading out and joined us on our search.

"Thanks for coming along Youramine. Maybe you'll see something out of the ordinary that we wouldn't."

"I hope so Sunny. We need to get to the bottom of this. We cannot live like this much longer, and you cannot stay here forever to play music for us."

We walked past the waterfalls, where I had been attacked the last time. After another quick search of the area, we followed the trail further into the jungle.

"Youramine, do you know where Tahoe has been for the last ten years?"

"Yes, we sent him to the land of Hondue. It is a place where people in our dimension can go to reflect on their wrongdoing."

"Like a prison?"

"No not really. It is a very enjoyable island. The people of Hondue are very nice. He was not confined to Hondue. He was free to go anywhere, but here. Although, he must return to Hondue at least four days a week."

"Can you contact anyone on Hondue to see if he was indeed there?"

"Yes, I suppose we can, but they would have contacted us if anything was wrong."

"Well, I'm probably barking up the wrong tree anyway."

John had the same feeling he had earlier, that someone was watching them.

"Youramine, do you think someone is watching us?"

"Yes, it is Tarek. He is supposed to protect you. Do not worry about him, he is a good man."

With that, Youramine raised her hand and a man walked out of the jungle and onto the trail just ahead of us. It was the man from the street and then Porkey's parking lot.

"Sunny, John and Curt, this is Tarek," Youramine said.

We all shook hands.

"I hope I haven't scared you too badly. I just wanted to warn you of the danger you might be in, here on our island. I am sorry I was not there when you were attacked at the water falls," Tarek said, bowing his head.

"That is okay Tarek. I feel safer now with you here," I said.

Youramine nodded at him and he disappeared back into the jungle.

We followed the trail another mile and came to an opening in the jungle, which had a small group of cabins around what looked like, and what probably was, a large distillery.

"This is where we make our Rum. We have another factory in the third dimension where we all live," Youramine said.

"Can we go in?"

63

"I will see. We do not want to spoil the process. We might have to come back."

Youramine walked to the building. Before she could get there, a man stepped in front of her and raised his hand for her to stop. They had a short conversation and she returned.

"He asked if we could come back in about an hour. It is a very tricky process making the special rum for us."

"That's fine. Let's go a little further and we'll catch this on the way back."

Another half mile down the road and Wanta Mea appeared in front of us.

"Sunny, I have come to walk with you for a while. Is that okay?"

"You know it is. You're always welcome, and wanted."

"If you will be with them for a while, I will go back to my chores," Youramine said.

"Alright Youramine, thanks for coming with us," Curt said.

She kissed all four of us and disappeared.

"Have you discovered anything yet?" Wanta Mea asked.

"No, but we're gonna look in the rum factory on the way back. If we can get in."

"Of course you can get in."

"No, they were in the middle of a process, which couldn't be disturbed and asked us to come back in an hour."

"They shouldn't be. I told them not to make any rum today. Our vats are full because no one is in the mood to drink very much."

"Maybe we should go back and take a look," Curt said.

We started back toward the compound. Wanta Mea reached out and took my hand in hers. I could feel the blood rush to my head. I knew she could tell I was blushing without looking at me. She can always tell what I want and what is going on in my world that would affect me when she touches me.

She smiled and then her expression changed. She stopped on the trail and squeezed my hand tighter.

"Oh no Sunny. Someone has kidnapped Lori from your island."

"Are you sure?" but I knew she was. She was never wrong.

"You must go and save her."

"Rose and Bonnie are there with her," Curt said. "They were going to spend a few days chilling."

"Do you know where she is?" I asked Wanta Mea.

"No, something is blocking my view."

We hurried back to the cabins, got our few things, and went to the dock. Paris had the seaplane pulled to the dock and was ready to tow us away from the island.

"You take the plane. It will get you there faster. I will watch your boat," Paris said.

I kissed Wanta Mea goodbye and got into the plane with Curt and John.

"Don't worry Wanta Mea, I'll be back to fix your island."

"Just save Lori," she said.

Paris dove into the ocean and took the rope and towed us away from the dock. When I looked back, there was only Wanta Mea and the dock. The island was gone.

Chapter 14

We landed in Marathon around noon. We taxied the seaplane to the marina and John jumped off onto the dock and tied us off. John had called Rose on our way in and she was waiting for us.

"Rose, what happened?" I asked. I could hear the urgency and panic in my own voice.

"We were up late watching old movies. Lori went to the kitchen to get us another bottle of wine. After about five minutes, I went to check on her. She was nowhere to be found."

"Did you search the island?" I said, knowing they did. The island is only twenty acres.

"We looked everywhere, but it was dark. We called Captain Burk in Marathon. He came with five of his men in a boat. They searched the island until well after daylight, but there was no sign of her."

"Was my dingy still at the dock?"

"Yes, and our boat too."

"And you didn't hear any boats approach the island?"

"No, nothing."

Rose started crying and John held her and tried to comfort her.

"I'm so sorry Sunny," Rose said through her tears.

"It's not your fault Rose. We'll find her," I said, trying to convince myself.

We went to the police station to talk to Captain Burk. He was a longtime friend of Johns and a new friend of mine. Burk was six foot four inches tall and around two hundred and fifty pounds. He was a very intimidating guy. Every time I was around though, he would have some kind of a crisis to take care of. He would probably be glad to see me move away.

He filled us in on his search and assured us he wouldn't rest until we found Lori.

Curt and I took my boat and cruised out to the island where Bonnie was waiting for us. From the water everything looked just as I had left it, the peaceful waving of the palm trees and the Rum City Bar sign to greet us.

"Any word yet?" she asked as we stepped to the dock.

"No, I was hoping you would have some good news."

We made another search of the island, but there was no sign she had ever been here.

In the house, we reenacted the night up to the point when Lori went into the kitchen.

"Was the wine bottle out on the counter or opened?" I asked Bonnie.

"No, she never got to the wine rack. Someone must have been waiting for her and grabbed her as soon as she came in the room."

The wine rack was across the room from the doorway she would have entered through. It was full except for one bottle, which was the one they opened first.

"It just seems impossible. No sign of struggle or foul play."

I walked around the kitchen, checked the windows and the door. They didn't look as if they had been tampered with.

"Was the door open when you came in to check on her?"

"No, it was still locked."

"Locked, how did they leave?"

"I don't know."

"Did you search the house good?" another stupid question, the house is only two rooms down and two bedrooms and a studio up.

"Yes, we went over and over every inch."

"Did you call Lori's cell phone?"

"Yes, it was lying on the floor by the pantry."

None of this made any since. How could someone just disappear? Then I thought about Rumora, they appear and disappear all the time.

I wish Wanta Mea were here.

"Curt, this might be way off base," I said, "but do you think it could have been someone from Rumora that was trying to get us off the island?"

"Maybe, but I don't think any of them could do anything like this," Curt said.

"Do you think you could fly back to Rumora and ask Wanta Mea to come here?"

"From what I understand if she leaves the island right now, she will lose her powers because of being weak already," Curt said.

"Yeah, I think your right," I replied.

"If we don't hear anything from Lori by tomorrow morning though, I'll fly back to Rumora and talk to Wanta Mea."

"Thanks, that might help."

"You know, I love Lori too, and it could have just as easily been Bonnie or Rose," Curt said.

"Yeah, I know."

Curt and Bonnie stayed on the island and I took the boat back to Marathon. We were supposed to contact each other if we heard anything. I pulled to the dock and tied the boat off and called Rose to come get me. It was a warm muggy night, the kind of night that Lori loved. She was cold natured. It made me miss her that much more and hope she was safe and warm.

Rose pulled up in her Bentley GT Speed. She was breathtakingly beautiful.

I climbed in and we drove around Marathon for a while just looking for some kind of a clue.

We passed the Sand Dollar Motel where Rose was held when she was kidnapped only two years ago, when some drug dealers had a score to settle with us. We got her out and now Eddie, Lori's ex-boyfriend, and also drug dealer, is spending the next thirty years in prison. Rose glanced at the motel but didn't say anything.

We turned onto the street, which John and Rose live on, and Tarek stepped out in front of us again. Rose managed to stop a foot shy of ruining his pearly white teeth.

"Damn, he's got to stop doing that," she said.

He walked to my side of the car and bent down, way down, to speak to me.

"I believe the Terrainiens have Lori."

"Who are the Terrainiens?"

"When you left Rumora, Wanta Mea contacted Hondue to check on Tahoe as you wished. She found out the island had been taken over by the Terrainiens six months ago."

"Who are the Terrainiens?" I asked again.

"They are a hostile race, which seek to take over all of our dimension. They invade islands secretly, and overpower the people. Then they bring their people to live there and make slaves out of the natives. They were given their name by our people. We took it from the word Terrain. Terrainiens are the collectors of land.

"Do you think they're trying to take over Rumora?"

"Maybe, we don't know, but it is a possibility."

"How do I find them?"

"You don't. They will find you."

"If you're right and they have Lori, is there a chance we'll get her back?"

"I don't think they will kill her. They will make her their slave. They probably want to keep you looking for her so you will not come to Rumora and play music. It makes us too strong."

Tarek disappeared again and I called Curt and told him about my conversation with Tarek.

"Okay Sunny, come pick us up and we'll fly back to Rumora."

Rose took me back to the docks where my boat was tied.

"Do you wanna come with me to get them?" I asked her.

"Do you have anything to drink onboard?"

"Only a full bar."

"Then I could use a boat ride."

We untied and pushed off. Rose fixed us both a highball while I maneuvered out of the no wake zone and into the gulf.

The air felt good and the drink is just what we both needed.

"When we met seven years ago, did you ever imagine we would be here, like this, trying to solve a mystery in a parallel universe?" I asked Rose.

"When I met you Sunshine, I knew nothing I would ever do with you would surprise me. You were wild and free and chasing the world. I knew you would catch it someday."

We looked into each other's eyes and didn't speak for a long awkward five seconds.

I looked away first. "Do you think we can find Lori?"

"We'll find her. I have faith in you, John and Curt. You guys have done a lot of things that seem impossible."

The dock came into view, none too soon. It wasn't like Rose to flirt with me, if that's what she was doing. I think it must be the stress.

Bonnie and Curt were waiting for us at the dock. They hopped on board as soon as I came aside. I pulled away and turned for John's house.

"We're going to need weapons when we go back," I said.

"I have an arsenal in my study," Curt said. "Let's pick out what we need as soon as we get back."

Rose and Bonnie didn't like it a bit, but they didn't have a better idea.

We took an assortment of assault riffle's and hand guns, and stashed them in the plane. John had some holsters, which we could hide on our bodies, since we didn't think it would be a good idea for the people of Rumora to know we were armed.

At the last minute I ran back in the house to grab two guitars.

"You never know," I said.

On the way in my cell phone rang. Distracted from the hurry I was in, I answered it without looking at the caller I.D. I stopped in my tracks.

"Sunny, help me," I heard Lori's weak voice say.

71

Chapter 15

When I returned to the plane John and Curt gave me a funny look.

"What's wrong," John asked. "You look like you've seen a ghost."

"I just talked to Lori on the phone. I think she's in Key West."

"She's okay then?"

"No, I don't think so. She said she wasn't sure where she was, but she thinks she is in Key West. She's locked in a room. I could hear loud music in the background, like a band playing. It sounds like she's in old town somewhere. There was a cell phone in a box in the room she's in. While we were talking she heard someone coming and had to hang up."

"Change of plan then, we're going to Key West," Curt said. "It's an hour drive, but I can get us there in fifteen minutes in the plane."

"You two take the plane; I'm going to take Bloodshot. If she sees him she'll recognize us and maybe yell out."

"Do you have her number saved in your cell phone?" John asked.

I hit the call button and the last number popped up. It was an 812 area code.

"This is weird," I said. "The area code is from Indiana where I was raised."

"Someone is really messing with us. That couldn't just be a coincidence," Curt said.

"It sure looks that way, but we have to follow our only clue anyway."

I got in bloodshot and started the engine. The passenger door opened and Rose and Bonnie climbed in.

"What do you two think you're doing?"

"We're going with you," Rose said. "We're the ones who lost her and we're going to help get her back."

"Not a good idea."

"Let's go Sunny your wasting time and we aren't getting out," Bonnie said.

I pulled out onto Sombrero Dr. and turned toward Highway One.

"The guys are going to kill me for bringing you two along."

"We'll protect you," Rose said, and put her hand on my leg.

She knew she had me then. I was a sucker for her charms.

WE turned onto Front Street in Key West's Old Town district and drove toward Mallory Square. We didn't have a clue what we were looking for, but we kept our eyes peeled for anything that might look out of the ordinary.

We turned left and drove down Duvall Street slowly. Rose called John to see where they were.

"We're on White Street, a block off of Duvall," John said.

"Tell him we're going to park on Duvall and walk the street."

Rose did.

"We," John said. "You mean you're here in Key West?"

"Sunny made us come with him," Rose said.

"Oh thanks for protecting me," I said.

John said, "Yeah, I bet. You two be careful."

We parked on a side street and walked back to Duvall. The street was crowded from the two cruise ships that were in port. I knew from the past that in a few hours the streets would be bare again when the ships left.

As we walked past Sloppy Joe's I could hear the band playing.

"That sounds like the band I could hear playing over the phone," I said.

We went inside and split up. I walked down the left side closest to the windows and Bonnie and Rose went up the middle toward the band. They were anything but inconspicuous. Every man, and most of the women, watched their every step.

I looked around for a door, which would maybe lead to a room where Lori could be, but there was none. Only the rest rooms and the office and equipment room in the rear, next to the stage.

Through another door was another bar.

We met back out front.

"Maybe she could be in one of the buildings nearby," Rose said.

"Possibly."

We walked the block. Every building on it had rooms over the bars. She could be anywhere, and if she were with the Terrainiens, she could be miles away by now.

As I looked from bar to bar something caught my attention about a half block ahead. Someone was waving. It was Lori.

"Girls look!" I said and pointed toward Lori.

Just then, someone grabbed her and pulled her back into an alley.

I ran as fast as I could toward the spot where she had been standing. My legs felt like they were made of lead, like in one of those bad dreams where you can't get away from the monsters.

As I turned the corner and into the alley, I came to a quick stop. The alley was only fifteen feet deep and no exit or doors. She had simply vanished.

Rose and Bonnie came up behind me.

"What the hell," Bonnie said.

"I don't know. Where could she have gone?"

I called John and Curt and told them what happened.

"How are we going to fight that?" Curt said.

"I don't know. They have some strong powers. One thing is clear though, they are trying to keep us here. They don't want us back on Rumora. They want us to see Lori so we'll keep chasing them."

Chapter 16

I told them I was going to get Bloodshot and drive up and down Duvall Street. They should spread out just in case Lori saw me and tried to get away from her kidnappers again.

When I got in, I pulled the gun from under the seat and laid it beside me within easy reach. The guns grip felt cold. It sent a chill through my arm to my core.

I drove toward the docks. When I passed Margaritaville I saw Lori again. A man with dark skin, who was about seven feet tall, was hurrying her down the street. She saw me and tried to break free from her captor. It was no use; he tightened his grip on her arm and pulled her closer to him.

I knew it was just another ploy to keep me here looking for her, but I had no choice other than to follow them.

I drove Bloodshot up on the curb, grabbed my gun from the seat, jumped out, and ran toward them. He drug her along with him at a dead run. She had no choice but to run too.

They turned into a crowded bar on a corner and I chased them inside. I had my gun in my hand and this drew the attention of the patrons drinking at the bar.

People were screaming and bar stools were flying as the patrons, drinks in hand, tried to get out of my way.

I saw Lori and her captor run out the side door and back onto the street. I followed close behind, my legs no longer feeling like lead. I was gaining on them.

I wished Lori would drag her feet or just go down for a second. That would be all I needed to catch them, but she kept running as if she didn't want to be caught.

They turned another corner and I was close behind them. When I turned the corner, they had vanished again. There were people walking in groups, laughing and looking in windows, but no Lori.

Then I saw a man sitting on a bus stop bench. He was about seven feet tall and had bronzed skin and long black hair. I slowly walked over to him. He looked up at me and grinned. He slid over and said, in an island accent, "Hove'a seat my friend."

"Somehow, I don't think I'm your friend," I said.

"You con be. Hove'a seat and listen to what I hove to say."

I sat down next to the big man. I never felt so small.

"Where is Lori?" I asked him.

"Ahh yah, Lori. Very fine-looking young lady. She will make ah good servant."

"What have you done with her?"

"I have done nothing with her, yet."

"If you don't turn her over to us right now, I'll . . . ."

"You'll what. Kill me. Ha!" He said, losing his accent.

"You have no power over me. You cannot harm me."

"We'll see about that," I said and pulled my fist back and aimed right at his face.

His hand came up quickly and engulfed my fist. I could not move it. He grinned again. "See."

He let go of my fist with a motion like throwing a baseball. I almost fell off the bench.

He continued, "We are a peaceful people ya' know, when we are allowed to be. Our only problem is that we do not hove a land of our own. Our people use up our natural resources too soon. We, for the lack of a better term, multiply too quickly," he said and laughed. "Now we need more land and we have decided to take over Rumora. It is a very peaceful island and the people are very attractive, as you yourself have seen. They will be easy to overtake, because they do not believe in war."

"I'll never let you take Rumora," I said angrily.

"Ah, but you will, and you will even help us. We are not going to change the island. It will still hove that wonderful rum and the music, which is its soul. The only difference is the people that live there now, will be our servants."

"You're crazy, I won't help you. As a matter of fact, I'll do everything in my power to stop you."

"I do not think so, Sunny. If you do not do as we say, we will kill Lori, and you can watch us do it. Would you like that?"

I felt sick at my stomach. How was I going to choose between Lori and Rumora. I loved them both.

"Can I see Lori?"

"Yes you can, if you help us," he said in a friendly tone.

"Now, I want to see her now."

"Later. Now you must come with me to Rumora and tell the people to surrender to us or they will be destroyed."

"No, I can't do that. What makes you think the people there will listen to me anyway?"

"They are weak. We made sure of that. That is until you came back and played your music. That almost cost us a month's work, but now that you are gone from the island, we have managed to make them weak again. It will not be long before they will start dying, unless they surrender to us and become our servants," he said with anger; his accent vanishing again.

"You are evil people."

"No, we are survivors. We do what we must do."

"I won't help you, no matter what you do."

The man rose and walked to a doorway in a building right behind the bench. He reached in and pulled Lori out by the hair. She was crying and I could tell she was in a lot of pain.

"I guess I will just have to kill Lori for you. Then I will return to Rumora and kill Wanta Mea."

He started laughing. It got louder and louder until people were watching us.

Then he stopped and the man drew Lori close to him and pulled a long knife out of his waistband. Before he could get it to her neck, I aimed the gun and pulled the trigger. I hit the man in the right shoulder; he spun around and let Lori go. She ran toward me blocking my view of the man. I side stepped her advance and saw his arm going back to throw the knife. I raised the gun once more and pulled the trigger. This time I hit the man in the chest and he went down.

He had a surprised look on his face as he fell backward landing with a thump.

I had drawn a crowd now for sure. Lori was hanging on my arm and crying. The crowd, about six people, moved with us as we approached the man lying on the sidewalk.

Lori bent down and touched the man on the neck. She pulled her hand back and covered her mouth as if to stop a scream.

79

I knew I was going to be in big trouble for this. Then the man just vanished. The people in the crowd all gasped and looked at each other.

"What the hell," I heard one man say.

"Did you see that?" another said.

"Nope, I didn't see nothing," one man slurred.

I took the opportunity to take Lori by the arm and lead her away from the crowd of people, who were still looking at the spot where the man had been laying. The people were so shocked, they didn't even recognize Lori and me.

We got in Bloodshot and slowly drove away so we wouldn't draw any new attention. I could see the crowd growing on the sidewalk where it had taken place. No one was paying any attention to us.

I slid the gun back under the seat. The handle now felt warm, making me feel safe.

"Lori, are you okay?"

"I think so, but it's hard to tell. I kept vanishing and reappearing in another place. What is going on?" she said, tears forming in her eyes.

"You were kidnapped by some people who are trying to take over Rumora. They didn't want me there so they took you, knowing I would come back to get you."

"I'm sorry. Thank you for saving me, but what will happen to Rumora?"

"I don't know. We need to get back there, but I don't want to leave you here again," I said, gently wiping a tear from her face.

"You don't have to go back. We have a choice. Isn't Rumora too strong for someone take over?" Lori said.

"No," I said.

"Please don't go," she pleaded.

"I need to call everyone else and let them know you're alright."

I did. We met at the southernmost point and the all hugged Lori.

"Thank god you're alright Lori," Rose said. "I'm so sorry I let them get you."

"It's not your fault Rose. You don't have any reason to be sorry," Lori said, hugging Rose again.

"I can't help it, I just felt responsible."

Bonnie hugged Rose and said, "I was there too Rose. There was nothing we could have done. We did the right thing by calling the police to help find her."

"I know your right. I guess it's all too much. Sorry everyone."

We all hugged Rose and told her not to worry about us so much. "We'll be all-right."

"Let's get back to Marathon and make a plan," I said.

Rose and Bonnie flew back with John and Curt. Lori and I had some well-deserved time together in Bloodshot.

Chapter 17

Back at John's house, we sat together in a circle and had a very colorful discussion about what to do to save Rumora, if we could, and to protect the women back here at the same time.

The general consensus, which the men didn't like at all, was to take the women with us, to Rumora.

"How are we going to protect them there any better than we can here?" I asked.

"I don't know that we can," John said, "but at least we'll have the opportunity to try."

"Okay, what do we have in our favor on the island?" Curt asked.

"We have Louie-Louie and Lucy, although I'm not sure what good they will do us. And we have the support of all the natives of the island," I said.

"Yeah, that's something, but we need more. We need a miracle," Rose said.

"Your right, we need a lot more than a thousand, or however many natives there are, who will not participate in violence, to help us."

"Do you think when I shot that man and he vanished, that he was dead, or do you think he just went away to fight another day?"

"Man, I don't have the slightest idea," John said, "but I hope he died."

"Yeah, sounds bad, but I hope he died too."

"Why don't we get a good night's rest and we'll meet down here for breakfast and discuss this."

Lori and I stayed in our old bedroom at John and Rose's house. We had a lot of good nights in this room and this one was turning out to be one of the best. Lori was very grateful that I saved her and she was showing her gratitude.

Finally spent, we fell asleep in each-other's arms and didn't move until morning.

When I woke, I could smell coffee, bacon, eggs, and Rose. I got up and went to the kitchen where I found all four.

"Good morning Rose."

"Good morning sunshine," she said with crooked grin and a tilt of her head.

That was my nickname she gave me the first night we spent together and she still used it when we were alone.

"Something smells delicious this morning," I said.

"That would be me," Rose said, grinning again.

"Yeah, I know that, but I was referring to the food."

"Oh yeah, that too."

I sat down at the table and she poured us both a cup of coffee and sat with me.

"So, did you give any thought to Rumora, or did you lose all concentration in that wild ride, you and Lori were on last night?"

"Oh, sorry, didn't know we were that loud," I said, feeling my face turn red.

"Just kidding, it was fine after I put my ear plugs in."

Rose never missed the opportunity to embarrass me when she could. I bet she's made more blood rush to my head than everyone else combined, and not just the one I think with.

"Well, my thought is that you girls go with us. I don't like it, but I don't see any other way. If they kidnapped one of you once, they can and will, surly do it again."

"I think your right, safety in numbers, so to speak."

The rest of the gang appeared in the kitchen one at a time, until we were all there. It was good to be with a group of friends when there's a crisis, but I relish the time I get alone with Rose.

Everyone agreed that the women would go with us, so after breakfast we started loading the plane again with guitars and guns. What an odd combination. One instrument to sooth and enjoy and the other to kill.

♫

IT was a quiet trip to Rumora. Not at all like the past trips, where we would party all the way there and bask, in the anticipation of being among the natives.

We landed safely in the ocean and waited for Paris to come and get us.

We floated for two hours. John repeatedly hit the air horn we brought with us. We didn't know what else to do. If Paris didn't come get us, we would never be able to get on the island. How does one barge in on an island in another dimension.

One doesn't.

"Maybe we need to fly around for a while and come back and land again," I said.

"Or, maybe we can get closer," John said.

"How?"

"Well the first time I came, when they found me drifting, I was about twenty miles from here. When I asked them how they found me, they said I almost ran right into them. Then when I was invited to return, they told me to come here just in case I was ever followed. They didn't want anyone to know where the island was, even if it was in another dimension."

"Do you think you can find the same location you were in the first time?"

"Yeah, I have it marked on the map, in code of course."

"Let's give it a try."

We turned the plane into the wind and took off. Curt flew according to John's directions, which he traced on the map with his finger, and we landed again in fifteen minutes.

"I think this is as close as I can get to the spot," John said.

We hit the horn three times and waited. Nothing. We felt so hopeless just floating out on the open sea. There was nothing we could do but wait.

85

A few minutes later a fog set in and we felt a slight bump on the plane. Then we saw that Paris was holding onto one of the pontoons.

"Help me," he cried.

I reached down, took his hand in mine and pulled him into the plane.

"I am sorry," he said, "but I am too weak to pull you to the island."

"Can we help?"

"Yes, I will direct you if you can help me pull the plane."

We tied three more ropes to the plane and the four of us dove into the ocean. We all took a rope and swam along with Paris, who was getting weaker.

"We are almost there," he said in a faint voice.

Then there we were. The island appeared in front of us. We helped Paris to the dock and then helped the girls off the plane.

Standing there on the dock we would have never recognized the place if we didn't know where we were.

The palm trees looked dead and the flowers had all withered. Paris wasn't the perfect specimen he had been either. He looked beat. Like he had fought all he could and then had just given up.

"Paris, what has happened?"

"The people are getting weak again. They are starting to turn on one another. Some fights have broken out. That is not like our people."

"Is there any music playing?"

"No, not since you left. Our music will not make any sound."

"Have you noticed any new people on the island? Maybe someone visiting from another island."

"No, only Tahoe, but he is from here."

John and Curt went back to the plane to get the guitars. They also stuck some guns in their waistbands and pulled their shirts down to cover them.

I took one of the guitars and played an old song. It sounded great. Paris stood straighter and actually grinned.

"I feel much better," he said.

Looking around the flowers and trees, which were within sound distance, were getting color back, and starting to grow again.

"Man, this island needs music all the time. Is it this bad in the third dimension?"

"Yes, maybe worse. The music you play here has the same effect on the third dimension in the same location. So somewhere there, the trees are growing. Someone will come soon to see what has happened."

And with that statement Wanta Mea appeared in front of us.

"Sunny, I knew it was you," she said and kissed me hard on the lips.

Then she put her arms around Lori and hugged her hard. "We were so worried about you. I am glad you are okay."

"Thanks to you, for telling Sunny what happened to me," Lori said, hugging Wanta Mea again.

Wanta Mea then made the rounds kissing and hugging everyone.

"You have brought your music back to the island."

"Yeah we have. We hope it's not too late."

"I don't think so yet, but there is not much time. We will start to die."

"Wanta Mea, do you know if it's the Terrainiens that are trying to take over the island?"

"Yes, I thought of that possibility."

"It was a Terrainien who had Lori. I got her back, but I had to shoot him to do it. When he fell, he disappeared. Do you know if he died or if he just left?"

"They are very strong. I do not know for sure, but I think he might have died. If he did, they will be very mad at you. They live forever as we do."

"Do you think it's possible, Tahoe is working with them? He was on the island, which was taken over, and the trouble started here when he returned."

"No, he would not do that to us. He loves us just as you do."

"Well, I have to look at all of the possibilities. I'm sorry I had to ask you that."

"That is okay, I have thought of that myself, but I just can't believe it to be true."

"One more thing, are Louie and Lucy still here?"

"Yes they are on the other side of the island. I talked to them today."

"How are they?"

"Lucy is strong. Louis is just fine. That is, for Louis."

"Well, we better do something fast or everyone is going to be too weak to survive. When can I go to the Sovereign One?"

"You may go tomorrow, but tonight will you play music for us at the bar?"

"Yes, but I think I had better start now. Maybe the people will be strong enough to survive until I get back from my meeting."

Wanta Mea and Paris took everyone to their cabins to stow their gear while I was setting up at the stage. The wires to all of the amps had been cut. I was trying to salvage enough of them so I could splice at least one back together. Some one really didn't want us to play. They didn't want the island to regain its strength.

Just as I was about to get one put together the lights went out. Someone had hit me hard on the back of the head.

When I woke up, Wanta Mea was holding my head in her lap and crying. Someone else was trying to bandage me. I looked up and saw Lori.

"What happened?" I asked through the pain.

"I don't know. When we came back you were lying here and your head was bleeding." Lori said.

I looked at Wanta Mea, "Don't cry, I'm okay."

"It is my fault. I should have never brought you to the island. It is no longer safe here for you."

"It's safe enough. Don't worry, we'll make it safe for everyone again."

"Sunny, there's one more thing," Curt said.

"What's that?"

"All of the guitars are gone. Whoever hit you stole the guitars and destroyed the amps."

"Oh no, that can't be good. We need to find who did this and fast."

Rose, Bonnie and Lori took me back to the cabin and helped me into bed.

"I'm just going to rest for about an hour and then I'll be okay," I told them.

Lori climbed into bed beside me and Rose climbed in on the other side. Bonnie stroked my head softly.

"Maybe I'll lie here for four or five hours," I teased.

"Boy, it didn't take long for you to start feeling better," Lori said.

"You all know how to bring a guy around."

I would have loved to stay right there all day, but even in my condition, I could feel myself getting an erection.

"I think I'm okay now. I believe I can get up."

"I think you're already getting up," Rose said and laid her hand on my stomach.

They all giggled.

"That does it," I said and tried to get up.

The pain was too much and I fell back down onto the pillow.

"I'm sorry Sunshine, I thought you were ready to get up," Rose said and they all giggled again.

"You girls are just cruel."

Curt and John walked in and saw us all in bed.

Curt said, "I think I got hit on the head too."

"Don't be trying to take some of my sympathy," I said. "I need the nurses right now."

"Lucky," he said.

John said they were going to walk the island again. "Wanta Mea's going with us. That is unless you need one more beautiful girl in that bed with you."

"Oh, do you think she could," I said.

"We've got him covered John," Lori said. "You guys be careful."

"Take care of Sunny. We'll be back in about an hour," John said and they left.

"Girls, I know Wanta Mea said she didn't think Tahoe had anything to do with this, but I think it's kind of strange that it all started when he showed up."

"Yeah, me too," Rose said.

"Is there any way we can spy on him?" Bonnie asked.

"I don't know how. He has a lot more powers than we do."

"Will Youramine help us?" Lori asked.

"That's a good question. She might. Do you think you can find her?"

"We'll try," Lori said. "Rose, will you stay here with Sunny? Bonnie and I can go look for Youramine."

"Sure, I'll make sure he behaves himself," Rose said, stroking my head again.

Lori and Bonnie both kissed me and left. I expected Rose to get out of bed now since the others were gone and this might be a little awkward, but she didn't. She just held me closer. I closed my eyes and drifted off into blissful sleep. The last thing I remember was the smell of her perfume.

When I woke, I saw Bonnie, Lori and Youramine staring at me. I smiled, and then I noticed an arm around me. I looked over my shoulder and saw Rose was asleep and spooning me. My grin got bigger.

"Well, I bet you feel better now," Lori said.

"Yes I do."

Rose woke up and looked disoriented for a few seconds. Then seeing everyone she smiled too and hugged me tighter.

"We better pry them apart and try to get Sunny up before he decides to never get up," Lori said.

The girls helped me up slowly. My head still ached a little, but to be honest, all I could think about was Rose holding me while I slept. I felt great.

Chapter 18

I finally forced myself to get out of bed. My head still hurt, but all-in-all, I felt pretty good.

"Youramine, do you think you can help us try to find out if Tahoe was on Hondue or not?" I asked her.

"I can help you, but I am feeling weak. I may not be as much help as I could have been."

"I'm going to try something, just to see." And I started to sing a soft song.

Youramine started to perk up a little. "Yes, that helps," she said with a smile. "I feel better already."

I sang for a few more minutes and she looked as healthy as she always had.

"Thank you," she said and kissed me.

"Okay, what's the plan?" I asked her.

"I think we should go to Hondue and find out what happened there. The Terrainiens took over the island. Maybe we can find out how, and at the same time find out why Tahoe was not captured by them and where he went."

"Can I go there?"

"Yes you can. If you hold me tight, we can go together. Do not let go of me until we get there or you may be lost forever."

"I'll do it. Can we go now?"

"Yes."

I told Lori to tell John and Curt what I'm doing, but don't say anything to Wanta Mea about Tahoe.

I put my arms around Youramine and held her tight. We vanished from the room. We traveled through a tunnel of blue and red cloudlike swirls. I felt as though Youramine and I were one. The tunnel had a calming effect on me. I totally forgot all about my worries and thought of nothing but pleasure. She turned in my grip and faced me. She put her lips to mine and kissed me long and soft. I could feel myself melting into her. Then we were naked and we were making love. I've seen her naked many times, but never like this. We were closer than I have ever been to anyone in my life. Her hair was flying in what looked like flames. Her eyes were deep and penetrated my soul. I felt her tongue in my mouth and I returned the gesture. When we climaxed, we were as one. I have never felt anything so powerful in my life.

The tunnel started to get a little brighter and turn a light shade of yellow. Then we were standing in a jungle and the tunnel was gone.

"We are here," Youramine said.

I just stared at her. She smiled at me and said, "You have quite an imagination."

I felt myself turning red. "Sorry, so I guess that didn't really happen."

"It happened."

I stared at her again. "Come we must hide," she said.

The island looked a lot like Rumora. The birds were singing and the flowers and trees were in full bloom.

We stayed behind trees in the jungle and worked our way through the thick overgrowth until we could hear the sounds of a village. We could see a young woman picking something in a garden.

"I know her, she is Toi. She is a friend of mine. I have stayed here with her family many times."

Toi was dressed in what looked like a flour sack. It must be the official uniform for the slaves.

"They used to dress in bright colors. They loved being free and dancing," Youramine said.

We got down and crawled toward her. When we were within speaking distance to Toi, Youramine called to her in a whisper. "Toi."

Toi was startled. When she saw who it was her eyes got big and she looked around. She whispered back, "You must go away."

"Can you come closer?"

Toi started working her way toward us picking as she came. When she was a few feet away, she stopped. We were still in the bushes.

"Youramine, why are you here?"

"I need to know what happened to your people."

"We were taken by the Terrainiens."

"Yes I know. How did they do it?"

"I think they had the help of one of us. They poisoned our food and made us weak."

"Was Tahoe here?"

"Yes, it all started shortly after he arrived. We thought it might be him, but we are not sure."

"YOU THERE, WHAT ARE YOU DOING?" A man's voice called.

94

"I am picking Tate for supper, my master," she answered.

"GET AWAY FROM THE JUNGLE."

Toi rose and walked back to the center of the field where she was when we arrived.

We sank lower and scooted back into the jungle.

"We must go now," Youramine said.

"What is Tate?" I asked her.

"It is a vegetable that the Terrainiens eat. It takes up all the nutrients in the soil and destroys the land. That is why they move from island to island. This island will last about two hundred years. Now we must go."

Just as I was about to put my arms around her, I felt a strong hand on my shoulder. I turned to see an enormous man standing there pointing a sword at my face. Another man grabbed Youramine from behind and held her tight.

"What have we here?" the one with the sword said. "I think we have just caught two spies. I don't think this one is from our world," he said looking at me.

I looked at Youramine. She could not move. Then I had a thought. "Youramine take him away and lose him and come back for me."

She nodded her head and they vanished.

The man holding me was startled and let me go. I turned and kicked him hard in the balls. I didn't like doing that but I didn't know what else to do. He went down and rolled on the ground.

Youramine appeared in front of me again.

"Did you lose him?"

"Yes, what did you do to this poor man?"

"I gave him a minor adjustment."

"Hold me tight and let's get out of here."

We vanished once more and entered the tunnel. Like before we were naked and joined as one. I thought of nothing but pleasure. I forgot about Rumora and Hondue. Nothing could ever feel this good. I could have stayed in her embrace forever. This time we came to a stop in the tunnel. I asked her what happened and she said she did not want it to end yet. We stayed there making love for a long time. Then we were moving again and the tunnel started to turn yellow and get lighter. Then we were standing in the cabin. The girls were still there.

"Thank god, you two are alright," Lori said.

"Did you tell John what we were doing?"

"No, not yet, you were only gone for a minute."

I looked at Youramine and she smiled at me. "Things move at a different speed in the suspended dimension between the second and third dimension."

"So what did you learn?" Lori asked.

"The Terrainiens did take over the island. A girl we saw there, a friend of Youramine's, said they think Tahoe may have had a part in it. Someone poisoned their food and made them weak. They can't prove it was Tahoe, but it did start shortly after he appeared."

"Just like here. So maybe Tahoe is poisoning our food," Youramine said.

"Maybe, or maybe it is someone else."

Just then, John, Curt and Wanta Mea walked in.

"Did you find anything?" I asked.

"Not really. We did find quite a few tracks in an area where no one has any business going. They were heading off toward the rum plant," Curt said.

"Wanta Mea, before you go I want to sing to you. It helped to make Youramine strong enough to take me to Hondue. We found out that the Terrainiens poisoned their food to make them weak."

Wanta Mea gave Youramine a dirty look. "Did she have you hold her tight?"

"Yes, I didn't want to get lost."

Wanta Mea hesitated for a moment and then said, "Yes, you were right to hold on tight. It is very dangerous."

I sang to Wanta Mea. She and Youramine both gained strength from it. Wanta Mea was in a better mood after that.

"I am sorry Youramine, I didn't mean to snap at you."

"That is alright Wanta Mea. I know it is just the island. It is turning us all sour."

Wanta Mea said she needed to go back to the third dimension to see Tahoe. "He will wonder where I have been all day."

She kissed me, and then the others. I thought her kiss to Youramine lasted a little longer than usual.

"I will come to get you in the morning Sunny and take you to the Sovereign One."

"Thank you Wanta Mea, and don't worry, we'll save the island."

She looked at me sadly and vanished.

"She's not herself," Lori said.

"None of us are. We all do things we would never do otherwise," Youramine said. Then she kissed all of us and left.

"Poor girls, I feel so sorry for them," Rose said.

"I know it breaks my heart. We must stop this invasion," Bonnie said.

Chapter 19

We decided to make some makeshift beds in one cabin and stay together. Safety in numbers. The girls slept in the bed and we made pallets on the floor. In the middle of the night, I thought I heard a noise outside, coming from the rear of the cabin. I shook Curt awake and put my hand over his mouth. He knew that I wanted him to be quiet, so I took my hand away. I pointed to the back door of the cabin. We stood and walked quietly to the door. I could still hear someone moving out there.

Curt went to the window, parted the blinds, and peeked out. He ducked back down quickly. He held up two fingers, indicating there were two people out there.

He whispered in my ear that he was going to go out the front door and sneak around back. I gave him a thumbs up.

I watched from the edge of the window. When I saw Curt behind the intruders, I opened the back door.

I had surprised them and they jumped back. One took a swing at me with something like a club and I ducked away from it. Curt jumped on him from behind and I hit him hard in the mouth. He went down without a fight. The other was a huge man. He was going to be trouble, even for two of us. I swung at him and missed, but that gave Curt the chance to retrieve the club the other man had held.

Curt hit him hard from behind. He went down and was out.

All of the commotion woke everyone else.

John helped us drag the big man into the cabin. We went back to get the other man but he was gone. When we went back into the cabin, the first man was also gone. He simply vanished.

"Shit," I said. "How are we ever going to fight these people and expect to win? Every time you hit one they vanish."

"I don't think we are," Curt said.

"Well I guess we had better sleep in shifts. I'll take the first one. I'm too wound up to sleep now anyway," I said.

"So am I," Curt said.

The others went back to bed. Curt and I played cards for a while and then I said I was going to try to get some sleep. I found that it was easier than I thought.

When I woke in the morning, everyone else was already up.

"Sorry, my head must still be slowing me down a bit."

"That's alright, I think you needed it, but you better get in the shower. Wanta Mea will be here soon," Lori said. "I think this could be dangerous. I wish you wouldn't go."

"I have to go. You wanna save the island don't you?"

"Yes, but I worry about you."

"I'll be fine," I said and kissed her softly.

I was in the shower shampooing my hair when I heard the shower door open. "I was hoping you would join me," I said.

99

"Yes, Lori said she thought it would be a good idea."

"Wanta Mea, sorry, I thought you were Lori."

"She will be here in a moment. I wanted to talk to you first."

I rinsed the shampoo from my eyes and turned to face Wanta Mea. God she was gorgeous.

"Sunny, you do not have to go to see the Sovereign One today. It could be a dangerous journey. We will have to ride Griffins to get there."

"I've ridden Griffins before. Remember when I lived here with you for five years?"

"Yes I know, but this time there may be war on them. They are very spirited animals."

Griffins are a mythical creature. They have the body of a Lion and the head and wings of an Eagle. I remember studying about them, when I was in college. Of course, no one had ever seen one, but they were in some of the ancient Greek books. They're a wild ride. They can be guided, but if they're threatened, they will attack. They have a mind of their own. When I lived here with Wanta Mea, I rode them a few times.

"Tahoe said he would go with me to the Sovereign One and find out what we can about the life of the island."

"No," I said, maybe a little too sharply. "It's just that I want to know firsthand. Just in case there's something I can do that your people can't."

The shower door opened and Lori stepped in. "Well?"

"No, he still wants to go with me," Wanta Mea said.

"I told you he would."

"I'll be just fine," I said.

"I will wait for you in the other room," Wanta Mea said.

"Don't go," Lori said. "This is like old times when everything was fun."

Wanta Mea stayed and we all made love to each other. I felt a lot better by the time we left the shower.

Wanta Mea said she would be back in an hour to get me. I told her I'd be ready.

"Lori, why do you let me make love to Wanta Mea? Doesn't that seem strange to you?"

"No. I know it should, but what happens here in a different dimension doesn't seem real to me. I have had fantasies of my own about Paris, and I like it when Wanta Mea and I share you. I guess I'm a little kinky."

"I love you."

"I know. I love you too."

"If you want to make love with Paris, you can."

"I know."

Chapter 20

Wanta Mea returned in an hour. She was dressed in a revealing flowered dress. Her hair was pulled back, and held in place with a ribbon.

"You look beautiful," I told her, and she did.

"Thank you. I wanted to look nice for the Sovereign One."

Everyone wished me luck and said they'll do what they could for the people here while we're gone. They were going to sing as a group to try to give them a little strength.

I put my arms around Wanta Mea and held on tight. We vanished and entered the tunnel. The tunnel had the same effect on me again that it had when I was with Youramine. As we went through, she turned and kissed me. We made love the way Youramine and I did, but I only thought of Wanta Mea. I didn't want her to pick up any vibes about Youramine. The tunnel lightened and we were standing in an opening surrounded by the island people.

Wanta Mea smiled at me and said, "That was very nice Sunny."

"Yeah, it was," I said, trying to catch my breath.

One of the island people I knew, their spokesman, came to me, wished me luck and thanked me for what I was trying to do.

I promised him I would try my best.

A man came to us leading two Griffins. They were huge animals and they fought the reins a little, as he led them to us.

On Wanta Mea's command, the animals knelt down and we climbed on.

She told me to hold on tight and she nudged her Griffin into flight. Mine followed.

We were flying at a very fast speed. These animals were incredible. They knew the direction we wanted to go, but they had to investigate everything we passed on the way. They would fly over the treetops, and then only five feet off the ground, going under trees. They would turn sharply and in unison. Wanta Mea pointed to a tower on a distant mountain. I assumed the tower was our destination.

The Griffin flew almost straight up as we got closer to the tower. Then they dove and circled as they descended. I looked at Wanta Mea. She was holding tightly to the reins and leaning forward. Her long hair was flying straight out behind her. She was a very tough woman.

The Griffins landed in a smooth, soft touchdown and walked a few steps toward the door at the base of the tower. They knew exactly where we were going.

They knelt again and we climbed off. Wanta Mea dropped the reins and kissed both animals. They rubbed their heads on her shoulder.

"Let's go. They will stay here until we return," she said.

As we approached the tower, the doors swung open. I couldn't believe my eyes. There, guarding the door was a horse, but not your typical horse, this one had the body of a horse and the torso and head of a man. I remember them from my Greek mythology class also.

They are called Centaur. Half horse and half man. The man is attached at the waist to the horse's withers where its neck would be.

"You may enter. The Sovereign One is expecting you," he said.

He had a full beard and was carrying a large sword in his right hand. He pointed the sword down the hall.

We walked down the hall. The tower was furnished in island décor. It was not what I expected from the exterior, which had a mid-evil look. We came to a second Centaur. He opened another door for us that led to a stairway.

"You will take the sixth of eight doors. If you take the wrong one you will not return."

Once inside he closed the door and we could hear it lock. We climbed the stairs. It was dark inside and we could barely see.

"Are you scared?" Wanta Mea asked me.

"Yep, are you?"

"Yep," she answered.

I thought that was funny since Wanta Mea always spoke so proper.

We ascended the stairs looking up as we went, trying to see what was around the next turn before we got there. The sconces on the wall offered little light and the stairwell was damp and cold.

The stones of the stairs were uneven and I was aware I could stumble at any time and maybe open the wrong door.

There was a musty smell and water was running gently down the wall and over the steps. I could feel moss growing on the wall when I touched it.

"What did he mean we would never return?" I asked.

"Quiet, I am concentrating on the doors," she said, ignoring my question.

We could see a light shining at the top of the tower. It was coming from under a door, which appeared to be the sixth door in the tower.

"Do we bow or what when we meet her?" I asked in a whisper.

"We look down at her feet until she speaks, then we look her in the eyes. Do not worry, she is a good person. She just has a lot of power."

We came to the door and realized there were two other doors. One on either side.

"Which one," I asked Want Mea.

"Give me a moment," She said, and closed her eyes.

She held her arms in the air, and swayed gently back and forth and chanted an eerie rhyme.

"Death don't come
Hear my song
Spare our souls
We belong
Show us the way
To your heart
One in three
Stand and part"

The center door glowed and it swung open. Another Centaur was standing there. This one was clean-shaven, younger, and very muscular. Quite handsome.

"Enter," he said.

The room was decorated in very colorful wooden furniture. There were huge tapestries on the wall and exotic birds, which were free to fly. Across the room was a magnificent throne, and sitting on the throne was a very stunning woman. She had blond hair down to her waist and a golden tan skin that looked like it was airbrushed. Not a wrinkle or worry line in her face. She looked to be about twenty-five years old.

I tried to take my eyes away from her face but I couldn't. Wanta Mea was looking down and I knew I should too, but I couldn't get myself to look away.

She smiled at me knowingly, "That is okay, you may look up."

Wanta Mea looked up. "Thank you for seeing us," she said.

"I hope it will be to my benefit to do so."

Then she looked at me again, "So, you are Sunny Ray, the man who has been such a big influence on the people of my island."

"Yes, I'm Sunny Ray, but I don't know about the influence. It seems the people of your island have been a big influence on me."

"You are a lucky man Sunny."

"Yes, I've been told that."

"So, do you have some questions for me?"

"Yes. I do. You, of course, know what is going on with the island. The Terrainiens have taken over Hondue and now have their sights set on Rumora. I want to find out what's making the people here weak. To do so, I need to know the history of the island. What makes it so dependent on music, and what would cause the music to stop playing."

"You seek a lot of answers," she said.

"It is for the good of the island."

She stared at me for a moment. I could tell she didn't want to give the secrets of the island to a mortal stranger. Then her face softened again and she said, "Very well."

"Rumora is a very delicate island. It has a fine balance of music and Rum. The Rum of the island is made from the Ora plant, which grows nowhere else in this world or any other. Our people came from another island thousands of years ago. Our scouts found this island on one of their expeditions. We try to keep our islands young by living on them from between five and ten thousand years. We will never give up Rumora, but the older people will leave and go to another island and start new. The difference between the Terrainiens and us is that we only go to deserted islands. We do not invade the sanction of others. We have taken the Ora plant with us to our new island, and are pleased to say that we have managed to grow them there. I am four thousand thirty years old. I will reign over the island until I am five thousand. I will then choose a successor."

Then she looked at Wanta Mea, "You my child are my first choice so far. You were always the strongest child of Reddie. Your mother is one of the most powerful women in our tribe. She was forced to choose a child to inherit her powers and she chose you. You will understand some day."

Wanta Mea looked shocked.

"You shouldn't look so surprised. You have proven yourself many times when the people of Rumora needed help or guidance. I have watched you."

"Thank you," Wanta Mea said and looked down again.

The Sovereign One looked at me again.

"That is just a little history so you will understand what I am about to tell you."

"Yes Ma'am," I said, trying to come up with something better than ma'am to call this lovely woman.

107

"The Rum of our island is quite magical, as you have discovered. It will make you strong, creative and give your soul a whole new rhythm, depending on which one you chose. The music on the island is fed by the Rum. It will not sound without it. The people who were born on Rumora are fed by the music. That is one drawback we did not see when we inhabited the island, but we have adapted well to it. Now the music does not play. You are an outsider so you can come here and play music. That will temporarily make the people of our island and the island itself strong. If you drink the Rum and it is poisoned, it will stop you from playing music. Without music, the people cannot survive. The island itself cannot survive without music now because it has become its soul. You know the trees and plants are living. They need nourishment. Music provides that. The Rum is the blood that runs through the islands veins. So Sunny, if you seek the beginning, it is the Ora plant."

"How can I tell if the Ora plant is compromised?"

"It will tell you. Just hold a leaf in your hand and close your eyes. When you open them you will know."

"I will take him to the Ora field," Wanta Mea said.

"You my child are so lovely, but I must warn you that the men in your life can be dangerous. I know that you love Sunny. He is a good man but he is not of our world. I would prefer that the leader of our people would be married to one of our own."

I turned red, and looked at Wanta Mea.

"Yes Ma'am," she said.

"But, if Sunny can save our island, I will consider him one of our own," she said with a smile.

Wanta Mea smiled. "Sunny has a girlfriend in his world already."

"Yes' Lori. She is a very wonderful young lady, but that can also be deceiving. He can have a wife in both worlds if he chooses to. Although Lori is a very sweet young girl, she has caused the delay of Sunny's progress. Please try to stay focused on the problems of the island."

Now Wanta Mea was red. "We have not discussed marriage, and there is Tahoe."

"Tahoe is not good for you. You do not need to feel obligated to him. I suspect he may have something to do with our troubles. Tread lightly around him."

"Thank you, I will."

"You two, be very careful returning home. There are some bad forces out there."

"May I ask you why you haven't gotten weak like the others," I said.

"I was not born here. Although I like the Rum and the music, my life does not depend on it. If the Rum is making people sick, I will still be alright. I haven't had any for a few months. I need to get out and have some fun, don't you think Sunny."

"Yes I do. Everyone needs to enjoy life."

"Maybe someday you can take me for a ride in Bloodshot."

"You know of Bloodshot?"

"I know of everything that affects our island and its people, but somehow someone has blocked this invasion from me."

Sensing our meeting was over I said, "Thank you for meeting with us. It's been a very enjoyable visit. I hope to see you again someday."

"I enjoyed our meeting also."

"How should I address you if we meet again? Ma'am just doesn't seem right for someone as young and beautiful as you."

"You may call me Corena. It is a very old name from our people."

"Then it was nice to meet you Corena."

"I also enjoyed our meeting," Wanta Mea said.

We turned to leave and Corena said, "Wanta Mea, don't let that one go. He is a charmer. They are fun."

Chapter 21

We were escorted back out by the Centaurs. The Griffins were still waiting where we left them. As we approached them, they knelt and we climbed on.

"Where to," I asked Wanta Mea.

"Let's go to the Ora field. It is here in the third dimension. There is also a smaller one in the same place in the second dimension, but this is our mother field."

"After you."

She nudged her Griffin and we took flight. It was such an amazing experience. The speed at which they accelerated made it hard to hold on. I watched Wanta Mea and saw how she locked her feet under the wings and leaned forward, so I did the same. She was fearless.

We flew over the trees again and occasionally under them. I didn't even try to control the flight. I just held on. We came upon a volcano and flew around it twice. I could see the molten lava boiling inside and an occasional spew of lava and fire shoot into the sky. Then we continued on. Wanta Mea had a big smile on her face and one hand in the air. She was screaming like a kid on a roller-coaster.

She pointed to a field ahead. It had rows of Blue, Red and Green flowers in it. The Griffins climbed once more and then descended in a circular motion. They landed next to the field, which was surrounded by jungle. We dismounted. The fragrance was overwhelming. It smelled like the Rum.

"We need to take a sample from each color and test it," Wanta Mea said.

"I picked a flower from the Blue and held it in my hand. I closed my eyes. I got the feeling I had the first time I drank the Blue Rum. My muscles relaxed, my face softened and I felt a slight tingle run through my body. When I opened my eyes, I knew the flower was good.

"It feel's good to me. Like the first time I drank it."

Wanta Mea tested it also. "Yes you are right."

I picked a green flower and followed the same routine. I had the feeling again. This time my imagination was going wild. I thought of song lyrics that I had written years ago and had forgotten.

"That one definitely worked for me," I said.

"Me too."

We did the same thing with the Red flower. It's the one that gives you soul and rhythm. I closed my eyes but nothing happened. Then I started to get a burning sensation in my hand. I dropped the flower and looked at Wanta Mea. She was dropping hers too.

"It is bad," she said.

"Yes, I got that feeling too."

"That makes sense, it being the one that controls the rhythm."

"You're right. We need to stop the people from drinking the red rum."

"But we still need to make the music play. It will not play without the Red Rum," she said.

"If I don't drink any Red Rum, I should be able to play. That is if I can get a guitar."

"I will find one for you, but we still have to fix the Red Rum. We cannot survive without it."

"That's why I couldn't play the last time. I was okay until I drank the Red Rum."

"Let's check the fields in the second dimension," I suggested.

We got back on the Griffins and directed our flight to the area we first entered the third dimension.

Flying low over some trees, I caught some movement off to my right. Someone was flying along with us on another Griffin. I pointed to him for Wanta Mea to see.

She gave me a warning look and nudged her Griffin to go faster. They did. I had to practically lie down to stay on.

An arrow flew past my head. I turned to look and saw three Griffins were chasing us. I spurred my Griffin again.

He got the message and took over. Wanta Mea said they did not like to be challenged. We flew straight up and did a complete roll over and charged at the aggressors. Our Griffins must have been superior to theirs. Mine spun at the last second and knocked the rider off the aggressive Griffin. I looked for Wanta Mea. I saw her battling the other two. She was making a series of turns and dives. I reined my Griffin in her direction. When he spotted the attack on his friend, all I had to do was hang on.

We hit the first one from behind and broke its wing. It spun to the earth. Wanta Mea had the second one on the run. Her Griffin would not stop until one of them was dead.

I raced to catch them, but they were well ahead of us. Wanta Mea disappeared around the volcano. When I got to the other side, I saw a Griffin and its rider plummeting to earth.

"No, Wanta Mea, please no," I cried.

Just then, Wanta Mea flew past me from behind and did a victory rollover. Her fist in the air.

My Griffin accelerated again and caught them. We flew very close together the rest of the trip. The Griffins were jazzed from the battle.

We landed where our journey began. Wanta Mea hugged the Griffins and kissed them, I did the same. They returned the affection.

A man came to get the Griffins from us and put them away.

"Give them their freedom for a few days. They will return," Wanta Mea told him.

"Yes ma'am."

"They are my personal Griffin. I raised them from birth. They are good warriors," she said to me.

"Yes they are, and so are you."

"Thank you, you are very good yourself."

"What did Corena mean by your mother having to choose which child to give her powers too?" I asked

"I do not know. I only have one brother. The men are not as powerful as the women are here. I did not know my mother was so powerful."

Wanta Mea looked at the ground and I could tell she was in deep thought. "I have always felt as though I should have had a sister to share my life with."

"I don't have any sisters or brothers. That is the way it is sometimes," I said.

"Yes I know, but sometimes I feel incomplete. Remember when I pulled you from that creek, which was about to drown you?"

"How could I ever forget that? We were only ten but I fell in love with you the first time you kissed me," I said, remembering how she smelled like honeysuckle.

"Well my memory is faint from that time, but I remember you quite well. I also remember having a younger girl traveling with my mother and me. I think possibly that girl was my sister. I never saw her again after that day," Wanta Mea said, a sadness coming to her voice.

"What does your mother say about her?"

"Nothing. She say's I imagined it."

"Maybe you did. Maybe you just wanted a sister."

"Maybe, I don't know."

"We better get out of here before some of their friends show up," I said.

I held her tight and we entered the tunnel. It was amazing as always. We made love for what seemed like hours, but I knew now it was only seconds.

Chapter 22

We appeared in the cabin and we were alone.

"I guess everyone is at the concert," I said.

"Let's go to the Ora field and we'll catch up with them later," Wanta Mea said, anxious to solve the mystery.

"Sounds good to me."

We walked the path toward the Ora field. The trees and flowers had recovered nicely. The singing must be working.

I had never been down this path before. It seemed to run parallel with the path, which led to the rum plant. The path was well manicured and lined with flowers of every color. We were heading toward the volcano. I could tell this one wasn't as active as its sister in the third dimension.

The path took a hard right and we entered an opening, which was filled with Ora plants. The field was as exquisite and vibrant as the other one, but much smaller.

"Okay let's try the red first," I said.

Wanta Mea picked a red flower and held it in her hand. In a few seconds, she dropped it.

"It is bad," she said.

"I was afraid of that."

"What will we do?"

"Let's follow the path on past the field and see what's ahead."

"There is nothing out there but jungle. It is land we reserve for the wildlife. We will farm it someday when we need it," Wanta Mea said.

"Let's look anyway."

"If you wish."

We walked the path, which was starting to narrow and become slightly overgrown. The birds were singing louder here and the vegetation was thicker.

"I don't think we can go much farther," Wanta Mea said.

I pushed on another fifty feet and came to an opening where people were working in a field.

Wanta Mea grabbed my arm and pulled me down. We hid from view behind a tree.

"I know those people," Wanta Mea said. "They are my friends from the island."

"And I know the plants they're farming. That's Tate. I saw Youramine's friend, Toi, picking them on Hondue," I said.

"They have started to take over the island and capture our people."

"Yeah, we have to stop them before it's too late."

There were armed guards watching over the workers. They had swords like the ones on Hondue.

We backed away slowly from our position and got back on the path. We were heading back toward the volcano when we heard some talking on the path ahead.

"Keep walking or you will die," a guard was telling the three prisoners he had tied to a single rope, which he was holding.

Wanta Mea and I dove into the underbrush and lay still. The prisoners walked past first with the guard right behind them.

When he got past us, I jumped out and hit him hard in the kidneys from behind. The pain took him to his knees. I grabbed his sword and ran it through his chest. He fell forward and lay there for a few seconds before disappearing.

Wanta Mea cried out in shock.

"Quiet," I said and put my hand over her mouth.

The prisoners were untying the rope that bound them together.

"Are you okay?" I asked them.

"Yes, thank you for saving us."

"Let's get out of here," I said.

We walked as fast as we could back to the open path we had arrived on. When we got to the Ora field, we paused for a moment.

"Where were you when you were captured?" I asked.

"We were at the pond swimming. We didn't see them coming. The next thing we knew they were standing over us with their swords and telling us to get dressed and come with them," one of them said.

There were two men and one girl. I asked her where the other men with the swords went.

"They told our guard to take us to the field and they would go capture more prisoners."

"Let's get back to the bar where the concert is and get some help," I said.

We walked the path back to the cabins and on to the bar. The vocal concert was still going and the people were dancing and laughing and drinking rum.

"We have to stop them from drinking the Red Rum," Wanta Mea said.

I went to the stage and held my hand up for them to stop singing. That drew everyone's attention.

"What's wrong Sunny," Lori asked.

"It's the Red Rum. It's been poisoned."

"Oh my god," Rose said. "I just drank some."

"It won't hurt you. It will just stop you from making music."

"Who did it?" John asked.

"The Terrainiens. They're on the island and taking prisoners."

I turned to the audience and made an announcement.

"Please do not drink any more Red Rum. The Terrainiens have poisoned it. So far, the Blue and Green Rum are still okay. The island has been invaded and we need to stop them before they take over."

The crowd, which was happy and dancing only seconds before was now sad and shocked. They looked at one another, a few of them hugged and a few wept.

"What do we need to do?" Paris asked from the front of the crowd.

"We are trying to figure that out now. We can fight them and win if we band together. Our numbers are greater than theirs right now, but not if we wait. They have taken over Hondue and made the people there their slaves."

"We cannot fight," Paris said. "It is forbidden."

"We either fight or die," I said, hoping to awaken something in them.

"We cannot fight."

I turned to John and Curt, "What are we going to do?"

"I don't know, but we better do it fast."

Wanta Mea stepped to the stage. "I have fought the Terrainiens. I had to battle with three of them today when my Griffins were attacked. I was victorious. They can be beat. Sometimes you have to fight for freedom. This is one of those times. We are not fighting each other; we are fighting for each other."

The crowd looked around at one another and there was some whispering.

"How do we fight?" One man asked. "We are weak now."

"We will work on that. I have an idea, but I have to talk with the Sovereign One again," I said.

I then turned to Wanta Mea and asked her if that was possible.

"I think so. What do you have in mind?"

"You remember her telling us they have successfully grown the Ora plants on a new island?"

"Yes."

"Well I wonder if we can somehow get some Red Rum from that island."

"Maybe. That is a good idea."

"Yeah, I just hope it is not too late."

Two Terrainiens were hiding in the jungle watching the action on stage. "We must do something before they get more rum," one man said.

"We have to stop the blond haired man. He is trouble. Tahoe said his name is Sunny."

The two men slid away from the edge of the jungle and walked back to the Rum Plant where there was a group of fifty Terrainiens working on the Rum.

"We have a problem," the man from the jungle said after he gathered everyone around.

"Sunny, the blond haired man, is going to get more rum from another island. We must attack now while they are weak."

"We are not ready for that yet," a big man said stepping into the room.

It was Rainier, the leader of the Terrainiens. He came to the island to see the progress of his people.

"If we attack now, more of us will be obliterated. Is that what you want? The man they call Sunny has already abolished two of our people. They will have to start their lives over now. They have lost hundreds of years."

The big man stood in the center of the gathering and looked at his people. "Have patience. Our time will come. In the meantime, destroy Sunny."

Chapter 23

Sunny and Wanta Mea stepped from the stage. Lori joined them at a table. John and the rest tried to sing another song, but the people were too distracted.

"What was the Sovereign One like?" Lori asked.

"She was a very nice person. Very attractive and young looking, but she was actually four thousand and thirty years old."

"Wow, I didn't know they lived so long."

"They can live forever. Wanta Mea will be the Sovereign One in another nine hundred years."

Lori looked at Wanta Mea, "Is that true?"

"Maybe."

"How old are you?"

"I am thirty five. I am a newbie, as you say."

"What will you look like when you are six hundred?"

"I will look as I do now. I will never age after twenty five, unless we lose our rum."

"Wow, I wish I had some rum like that at home," Lori joked.

"As long as you drink it while you are here it will keep you younger than your friends."

The island had regained some of its soul. The smell of honeysuckle was in the air again.

Bonnie came and joined us at our table.

"It doesn't do any good to sing now. The people are worried about their future," Bonnie said, "and I don't blame them, I'm worried about them too."

"I think we should go now," I said to Wanta Mea.

"Yes we should. I will come and get you in one hour."

"I'll be ready."

"Be careful until I get back. You have some strong enemies on Rumora," she warned.

"Yes, I do seem to have made some enemies."

Wanta Mea disappeared and left Bonnie and I standing there silently pondering our situation.

"Will she do it? Will the Sovereign One help you to get some rum?"

"I don't know. She should, to help her people, but she stands on tradition also. That means no violence and no outsiders."

Curt, John, Lori and Rose joined us.

"Well so much for a vocal concert or any other kind. Without the Red Rum, these people have no interest in music. At least when they thought they were drinking Red Rum they acted interested," Curt said.

"Yes, it's like the idea of Red Rum was at least something, but without it they're lost," Rose said.

"I'm going to see the Sovereign One in an hour. Maybe she'll let us get some rum from another island where they've grown it."

"We can only hope she'll do the right thing."

Wanta Mea appeared in her living room. She loved her house. It was decorated by her mother Reddie, and herself. Her father helped with the construction of furniture and the room she added on last year.

Magnificent tapestries she bought in Hong Cong last month hung from the twenty-foot walls. Flowers of every color grew in mosaic pots she had scattered around the house. She thought of losing all this to invaders and a chill ran through her body.

"Where have you been all day?" Tahoe asked surprising Wanta Mea, she did not know he was here.

"I have been to see the Sovereign One, and what are you doing in my house?"

"I told you I would go with you. Did Sunny go with you?"

"Yes."

"Where is he now?"

"He is waiting for me. We are going to see her again."

"I forbid you to go with him again."

"You cannot forbid me anything. Do you forget my powers are greater than yours," Wanta Mea said in a slightly louder and a lot more forceful voice.

"Maybe, but Sunny's are not," he said and vanished.

Wanta Mea stood in her living room and wondered what if anything Tahoe might do. She needed to warn Sunny.

Lori and I returned to our cabin to unwind. She thought it would be a good idea if she gave me a massage to help me release some of the tension that had visibly built up in my body.

Everyone else said they were going for a walk to the Rum Plant to see if anything out of the ordinary was going on. Since they didn't know what was ordinary, Youramine accompanied them. John had his gun and said they would be safe.

Just as Lori was getting down to the part that would really relieve my tension Wanta Mea appeared.

"Oh, I am sorry. I didn't mean to...."

"That's okay. I thought we had more time. We were just, uh, unwinding a little," Lori said.

"I came to tell you that Tahoe is very mad at you for going with me to the Sovereign One. He might try to hurt you."

"Wanta Mea, he wouldn't be mad at me for just doing that. You have to accept the idea that he may be working with the Terrainiens like she said."

"I know you are right. I just don't want that to be true. I would feel partly responsible for all the trouble."

"You're not responsible for any of the trouble. You're one of the only ones who's trying to save the island."

Wanta Mea sat down on the bed and put her head in her hands.

"Why can't life be the way it was? I miss all the good times we have."

"We'll have them again. I promise you," I said hugging her.

I got up and dressed. I felt a little funny talking seriously with these two women while lying there naked.

"Are you ready to go?' I asked her.

"Yes, the sooner the better."

Chapter 24

Wanta Mea and I arrived back in the third dimension once more. It looked to be in a healthy state.

"The music our friends made in the second dimension, worked here too," Wanta Mea said.

We were met by the same man leading the Griffins to us.

"These are fine animals Wanta Mea. I saw you were coming back early and all I had to do was whistle and they came back home," the man leading the Griffin said.

"Yes, they love to be ridden. It is bred into them."

The animals knelt down as soon as they arrived and we mounted them again. I could feel the tension in their breathing through my legs. They were slightly quivering. I knew they were ready to fly and probably hoping we would do battle.

With a slight nudge, they took flight. The experience was as exhilarating as it was the first time I flew. The Griffin took charge of the journey and we were just there for the ride.

We could see someone following us off to the right, but they kept their distance and didn't engage us.

We landed safely at the tower and were greeted by the Centaur.

"I am sorry Wanta Mea, but the Sovereign One will not see you today," he said.

"Why is that? We need her help to save the island."

"The island cannot be saved today I am afraid. You must come back next week."

"Next week might be too late. We must see her now," Wanta Mea said and took a step toward the door.

The Centaur stepped in front of her and held his sword up to stop her.

"Please Wanta Mea, if you love the island, come back next week."

"It just doesn't make sense. The Sovereign One would want to help us."

"Yes, and I would like to help you too, but not today. Now leave."

"Come on Wanta Mea. We'll figure something else out."

We mounted the Griffin and sat there for a long moment watching the Centaur. He looked pained to have to send us away, but it was obvious he was not going to change his mind.

The Griffins were acting a little different. They seem to be sensing fear or trouble.

"Something is not right," Wanta Mea said.

"Yes, I picked up on that too. Let's ride away and stop and talk this over."

From the window of the Sovereign Ones room, Tahoe watched the two ride away.

He nodded to his men who were holding her at sword point. They threw her on the floor and tied her to the legs of her throne.

"Remember, we will kill Wanta Mea and Sunny if you let them have any more rum from another island. Then we will kill you and your Centaur as well," Tahoe told her. "It is better to let your people live to serve us than to let them die."

We flew away and landed in a field a couple minutes later. The field was covered with some kind of vine that looked to be alive. It was moving in a snakelike motion.

"What is this?" I asked.

"This is Toran Root. We use it for healing. It will not hurt you."

Wanta Mea took a small purse from around her neck, held it close to the ground, and opened it. Pieces of the Toran Root separated from the vine and jumped into her purse.

"Just in case," she said and returned the purse to her neck.

I still didn't like it, but what do I know?

"So, what do you think the problem is at the Tower? The Centaur didn't seem to want to make us leave, but it was more like he didn't have a choice."

"I know. It is not right. Something is wrong there."

"Is there another way in?"

"Maybe through her window, if we can get there."

"Let's try. Maybe we can at least see in the window."

We flew back in the direction of the tower. As we approached, we saw two men on Griffins flying away. We recognized them as Terrainiens.

"Look," I said pointing at them.

That was all it took for our Griffins to attack. I held on tight as we overtook them. They saw us coming and drew their swords. They turned to face us and we maneuvered around them. We were doing a ballet in the air. Circling each other we would try to charge them and then have to dodge away to keep from being cut from their swords.

"Wanta Mea, I'm sorry to have to do this," I yelled at her.

I drew the gun from under my shirt and shot one of the men in the chest. He fell off and plummeted to the ground.

His Griffin, however did not give up the fight. It attacked mine and a battle started. Lion claws were ripping at the air and I was in danger of being sliced to pieces.

My Griffin once again proved his superiority over his enemy. He reared up and came down with a mighty blow decapitating the other Griffin.

Wanta Mea was still dancing with the other Terrainien. She was holding her own but was no match for a sword.

I turned my Griffin toward him and charged. We caught him broadside with his sword raised to attack. He swung it down and I ducked just in time to keep from losing my head. My Griffin opened its beak and tore the head off the rider. It was a gruesome sight to see.

Wanta Mea put her hands over her eyes and looked away.

"Are you alright Wanta Mea?"

"I can't take any more of this. It must stop," she said anguished.

"I wish it could, but I'm afraid there's more to come in order to save the island."

Then she straightened on her mount and her eyes had a different look in them.

"Yes, you are right. Some have to die, so some can live."

I hated to hear her say that. That's something you would hear in our world, not theirs.

She turned her Griffin and took off toward the Tower. The window to the Sovereign One's room was on the back side of where we were. I saw Wanta Mea disappear around the building. I was close behind her.

She flew in slowly from below and hovered just below the window. I stayed back so as not to give us away.

Wanta Mea guided her Griffin upward slowly until she could see in the window. Then she ducked back down.

She pointed at the window and motioned that someone was in there.

Then she stood on her Griffin and ordered it to rise to the window again. When she got level to the window, she dove through it.

I was in shock. I flew to the window as fast as I could and looked in. Wanta Mea and Tahoe were in heavy battle. I saw her throw him over her back and across the room. He landed on the floor with a thump.

He was up and coming at her again. She swung her arm back and forward again and the air between the two of them suddenly turned thick and wavy.

He flew across the room as if a cannon ball had hit him.

I jumped through the window and ran to her to help, but she didn't need any. Tahoe was not going to get up. His body looked broken.

I saw The Sovereign One tied to her throne and went to her to untie her.

"Are you okay?" I asked her.

"Yes, thank you for saving me."

I turned to Wanta Mea. She was still standing there looking at Tahoe. I walked to her and put my arms around her.

"We don't have time to hug. We must save the island," she said in a voice I had never heard before.

I could tell the event was already taking its toll on her.

"Wanta Mea, you had no choice but to do what you did. He was going to kill the Sovereign One."

"I have never hurt anyone from my island, but now I have blood on my hands," she said in a weak defeated voice.

"You had to do what you did," Corena said, reaching out to comfort Wanta Mea.

"Wanta Mea, what did you do? How did you hit him like that?" I asked.

"It is a power we have. We do not like to use it. It is bad."

"How did the Terrainiens capture the Sovereign One? Why didn't she use her power?"

"I can answer that," Corena said. "They said they would kill you if I worked with you. I was only waiting for the right time. When I could destroy all of them."

"Can you use it to protect the island?" I asked Wanta Mea.

"You don't understand. We do not want to use violence!" She said, her voice rising.

"Okay, I'm sorry," I said trying to calm her down.

"Wanta Mea my child, we must. We have used it in the past to defend our people. We just don't use it on our own people," Corena said in a sad voice.

Tahoe moaned and moved a little. The sound was weak, but he was alive.

"He's still alive," I said.

Wanta Mea went to him and bent down. She took his head into her hands and raised it.

"Tahoe, why did you forsake our island? Why did you force me to do this to you?"

131

"They exiled me from the island. The fight was not my fault, but they would not listen. I wanted revenge," he said in a weak whisper.

"I am sorry," Wanta Mea said. She laid his head back down gently and walked to Corena.

"What would you like for us to do with him?"

Corena thought for a moment and said, "I will summon the healer. He will take care of him. We will keep him in custody until this is over and then we will have a trial."

"Very well Sovereign One. Now we have a request of you."

"What is it my child?"

"We found that the Red Rum has been poisoned. You said it has been successfully grown on another island. May we get some rum from that island for our people?"

"I am sorry but that is not possible. It is like the rum on this island. It cannot leave the island. It will be poisoned also."

I felt my hopes drop. I was really counting on this being the answer. There had to be a way.

"Corena," I said, "can we grow more here?"

"It takes too long. The people will be too weak by then and will probably already be servants."

"This is really bad. Aren't there any other Ora fields on the island?"

"No, but did you only check the flowers in one row?"

"Yes, and only one flower."

"The Terrainiens know that the island needs the Red Rum to survive. The island will be of no use to them if all of the Red Rum is gone," Corena said.

"Your right. They have to have Red Rum."

"We must go back to the Ora field and check more plants," Wanta Mea said.

"Wait," Tahoe whispered. "There are still a lot of good plants in the field, but the field is booby-trapped."

132

Then Tahoe lay back down and was silent. I went to him and checked his pulse.

"His pulse is weak."

Just then, the Healer walked in. I didn't even know she had called him.

He went to Tahoe and laid his hand on Tahoe's chest. Tahoe stirred slightly and then opened his eyes.

"He will be alright," the Healer said.

I turned back to Wanta Mea. "How will we get the good flowers from the field with the traps planted in there?"

"We will find a way. Let's go," she said.

We bid farewell to the Sovereign One, and she wished us good luck.

We went back down the stairs and through the tower to the front door. We were escorted by Corena's personal Centaur. When we arrived at the door, it opened and the Centaur that had sent us away was holding our Griffins.

"I am sorry I had to make you leave. I was only protecting the Sovereign One. They would have killed her if I let you in."

"That is alright. She is fine now," Wanta Mea said.

A young girl watched all this from her hiding place in the jungle. She had hatred in her eyes. "I will get you two for this," she promised herself.

We mounted our Griffins and flew to the Ora field. Wanta Mea swooped down to the field only a foot above the flowers. As she flew over them, she slid down to the lion's leg, reached down, and plucked a flower from the center of the field.

We landed twenty yards from the field and tested the flower.

"It is good. The Red Rum flower is good," she said excitedly.

She put the flower in her mouth and ate it. I could see color coming to her face. She took on a much healthier look.

"Can you eat the flowers instead of turning them into rum?" I asked.

"The benefit will only last a short time, but I did not want to waste it. The rum helps us to make music and the music makes the island come alive. Everything must feed off of the other."

"Let's get back to the second dimension and check the fields there. Maybe with the help of the others we can find a way."

We mounted the Griffins once more and flew to the portal. This time there were no enemy attacks.

"Maybe we scared them," Wanta Mea said.

"Maybe. I know if they saw your power and my gun they are wise to be scared."

We turned the Griffins over to the keeper once again and I held Wanta Mea tight. We entered the tunnel. This time our lovemaking session was more intense than before. It must have lasted for hours. I could tell she was more aroused and eager to please. I knew there was a reason, I could feel it, but while we were entangled, I could not remember anything that took place outside the tunnel.

The light turned a soft yellow again and we were standing in the cabin.

"Where is everyone?" Wanta Mea asked.

"I guess they are still with Youramine looking for a solution at the Rum Plant. Lori might be at the bar."

Chapter 25

Wanta Mea and I walked to the bar. The path was covered with flowers, but they weren't brilliant in color, as they should be.

"The effect of the singing is starting to ware off," she said.

"Yes I see that, and it's awfully quiet around here too."

We entered the bar area and found ourselves alone. A few chairs were turned over. Cups and plates were scattered on the floor.

"Something has happened. There has been trouble here." Wanta Mea said.

I called for Lori, "LORI," but got no answer.

We walked the path toward the dock. Paris was sitting in a chair on the dock. Curt's seaplane was still tied there and Paris seemed to be watching it. As we got closer, we could see blood on Paris's face and down his neck. His eyes were closed.

Wanta Mea ran to him felt his neck for a pulse.

"He is alive, but he is weak. Someone has hit him on the head," she said, running her hands over his body looking for other injuries.

Wanta Mea withdrew a piece of the Toran Root and rubbed it on Paris's lips. He woke and opened his mouth. She placed the rest in his mouth and he ate it. He began to recover quickly.

"Paris, what happened?" I asked.

Paris looked around as if he didn't know where he was and then focused on me. A slight smile came to his face, but it was quickly replaced by a frown.

"We were attacked. I could hear the villagers at the bar screaming. When I got up to go help, someone hit me from behind."

All I could think about was that Lori was here with them. If they took the others prisoner, then they probably took her too. My mind flashed back to the first time I met her in Nashville. She looked so beautiful on stage singing her heart out for anyone who would listen. I felt responsible for her now, since I brought her here and put her life in danger.

"We need to go to the Tate fields and see if they have everyone held there," I said.

"We will need help. We cannot fight their whole army," Wanta Mea said.

"I have my gun and you have your power."

"My power is not enough. Once I use it, it takes an hour or so to recharge."

"Well, let's go and see if we can find them. Then we'll figure out what to do."

"Paris, will you be okay if we leave you?" Wanta Mea asked him.

"I am going with you," he said. "My head feels better already."

He got to his feet and lost his balance and fell back a few steps.

"No Paris, I think you should stay here and guard the plane, we may need it," I said.

"I am sorry I let this happen," he said.

"This isn't your fault. They are violent, and will use weapons to get what they want. We'll find them."

"Find Lori too. She was with me when the attack started," Paris said.

Paris sat back down and looked at us, "You find them, I will heal and then I will help you fight them."

"You've got a deal."

Wanta Mea and I took the path toward the Rum Plant and the Tate fields.

"Wanta Mea, whatever happened to Tarek? He was supposed to be watching over us from the jungle."

"I have wondered about that also. I fear he might have been one of the first to be captured."

"Did Tahoe know about him?"

"Yes, he is the one who appointed him to guard you."

"That explains a lot. Well, it's too late to do anything about that now. I hope Tahoe didn't do too much damage to the Rum Plant with the poison."

We walked on another hundred yards and then slid into the jungle to avoid being seen on the path. As we got closer to the Rum Plant, we could hear talking. There were guards around the plant. Big men with swords. They were laughing and drinking from silver steins.

Then we heard one of them call for more Rum. A young girl came with a tray of new drinks. It was Layme. The last time I saw her she was with John Denver at the bar and we were singing and having fun.

The men took the drinks from her and then one of them grabbed her and kissed her roughly. She pulled away and spat on the ground. They all laughed and she turned and went back inside.

"It looks like they have already taken over the second dimension. They will be taking the third dimension soon," Wanta Mea said sadly.

"FOOD" one of the men yelled. Another girl brought a tray of leafy vegetables to the men.

"That is Tate, it makes them strong. It is to them as rum is to us."

"Yeah, I saw them growing it on Hondue," I whispered.

We sank back into the jungle, skirted the rum plant, and worked our way around to the trail beyond and toward the Tate field, which we had discovered earlier.

As we got closer to the field, we moved into the jungle again. We crawled toward the edge and lay down flat. There were workers in the field, a lot of them. Guards were standing around the edge of the field calling commands to them and laughing.

I spotted Lori and Rose working close together, and then John and Curt on the other side.

"Do you see Bonnie?" I whispered to Wanta Mea.

"No, not yet."

We watched a few minutes longer and then we saw Bonnie bring the guards more rum. They took it from her and then put their hands on her breasts. She slapped one of them and he hit her and knocked her down. Curt jumped up and ran toward her, but he was intercepted by another guard with a sword.

Bonnie got up and spat at the guard who only laughed and said, "I'll deal with you later."

Bonnie returned to a tent where the drinks and food were and Curt returned to work in the field.

"We have to get them out of there soon. They will not succumb to the commands of the Terrainiens the way that our people do. They will get hurt," Wanta Mea said.

We moved back into the jungle deeper this time. We came to a small clearing next to a creek and drank some water.

"How are we going to get the flowers to make some rum and get the prisoners free, without help?" Wanta Mea asked.

"There has to be a way. They must have a weakness."

I thought for a minute, "Didn't you say that the Tate was to them as the rum is to you?"

"Yes that is right."

"Maybe we can poison the Tate. That would make them weak and then we could take over again."

"That might work, but we have no poison and I'm sure their poison is safely locked up and guarded."

"Yeah, you're probably right."

"If Curt was free we could fly back to Marathon and get some."

"You do not know how to fly?" Wanta Mea asked.

"No, afraid not, and you can't leave the island."

"No, afraid not," she copied.

"Amelia, she can fly you!" Wanta Mea said excitedly.

"You think she can still fly?"

"Sure she can."

"Do you know where she is?"

"Yes, I visit her sometimes. Come, I will take you there."

Chapter 26

After a long walk into a part of the island I've never been before, we came upon a small village of spectacular cabins. The trees were in full bloom as were the flowers. The trail was neatly maintained and people were talking and visiting with one another.

"Why's everything look different here?" I asked Wanta Mea.

"These are the people that have chosen to live here. They are not from our world, but yours. They do not need as much rum as we do for survival. They probably do not know we are having trouble."

I sure hoped they didn't know. I would hate to think they haven't offered to help.

We walked into the center of the village and were immediately greeted by some of the people living here.

"Wanta Mea, so glad you came to see us. I see you brought Sunny Ray with you. Great," a woman said. She looked very familiar.

"Sunny, this is Patsy," Wanta Mea introduced.

Oh my god, now I recognize her.

"Nice to meet you Patsy," I choked out.

"Nice to meet you Sunny, I heard you playing at Rum City Bar one night. You're very good," she said in a country draw.

"I've heard all of your songs. I love them," I said like a star struck kid.

"Patsy, we are having trouble on the island. Terrainiens from another island are trying to take it over and we need help," Wanta Mea said.

"Oh my god," she said putting her hands to her cheeks. We'll do anything we can. We're nothing without you and we owe everything to you."

"Where is Amelia?"

"She is down at the pond swimming."

"Thank you. I need to talk to her."

We started for the pond and Patsy Kline yelled to us, "Just tell us what to do, and we will help."

"Thank you," Wanta Mea called back.

We walked another path to a scenic waterfalls, with a turquoise pond at its base. Palm trees flanked the pond and several people were swimming in it.

"Amelia," Wanta Mea shouted.

Amelia looked our way, waved and then swam to the edge of the pond and got out. She was naked and had a very athletic body. She hugged Wanta mea and then turned to me. "Sunny, how are you?" she said and then hugged me.

"I'm fine Amelia, but we need your help," I said, feeling myself turning red.

She looked taken aback. "What could I possibly do to help you?"

"Do you think you can still fly?"

Her face brightened and her white teeth gleamed in the sunlight.

"Really, you want me to fly?" she said excitedly.

"Yes, if you think you can."

She threw her arm around me again and hugged me tight. "I've been waiting for a chance to fly for ninety years. You bet I can fly."

"I need you to fly me to Marathon Key Florida. Rumora is in trouble and I need to get some poison to try to save it."

"Is there anything else I can do to help?"

"Maybe, we don't know yet. I'll fill you in on the way there."

"Okay, ready when you are."

"I think you should put some clothes on first," I said, finally turning my head away.

"Oh yeah, you're probably right. You're turning red Sunny," she teased.

We walked back to Amelia's cabin and she dressed in her aviator clothes. They were the same ones we have seen all these years in pictures of her last flight.

"Okay, I'm ready if you are," she said excitedly.

We walked toward the docks on the other side of the island keeping to the jungle and ducking when we would hear any voices. We finally arrived and Paris was waiting there.

"Paris, how are you feeling?" I asked.

"I feel good now. Thank You for attending to my wound."

Then he smiled when he saw Amelia. "Amelia, give me a hug. What brings you here?"

She hugged him and pointed to the airplane. "That I guess. It's beautiful. They have changed a little over the years."

"The basics are still the same," I said. "You won't have any trouble flying it."

"Where are you going?" Paris asked.

"The Terrainiens have captured everyone including Curt and we need poison from our world. We are going to poison their food like they did yours."

Paris smiled again, "That's a very good idea. I think I like that."

"We'll need you to watch for us when we return. It should be tonight."

"I will come and get you. Just land where your GPS shows you that you are when you take off."

"GPS," Amelia said.

"Global positioning system," I said. "I'll show you. I do know how to work that."

"Okay, I'll fly, you do the rest."

I kissed Wanta Mea goodbye and told her to stay with Paris. I didn't want her to be captured too.

"I will be safe. My powers are greater than theirs are. You be careful."

"I'm in good hands. I'm not worried at all."

Amelia climbed into the pilot seat and I climbed in next to her. She looked around the cockpit at all the instruments.

"Wow, things have changed."

She read some of the instruments and was relieved. "These are just telling me things I had to know before without the help of a dial. Piece of cake. Are you ready?"

"Let's do it."

She started the engines and smiled when they came to life. She leaned over and kissed me again. "I'm happier than I've been in ninety years."

We taxied away from the dock, turned into the gentle breeze and looked to our right where Wanta Mea and Parris were. The island was gone, but Paris and Wanta Mea were still standing on the dock waving at us, a slight fog enveloped them.

Amelia ran a few tests and pushed the throttle forward. The plane came to life and we were skimming the water in no time. She slowly pulled back on the yoke and we were air bourn.

I wrote down the reading on the GPS and explained it to her.

"Well I'll be damned," she said. "What will they think of next?"

I thought of all the things I wanted to show her, but I knew I wouldn't have the time.

She handled the plane perfectly. I showed her how to follow the GPS and she caught on right away.

"Go ahead and make some maneuvers, we'll get back on course easy enough." I told her.

She turned right and then left, made a climb and a dive, her grin growing bigger with every move.

"This is great," she said. This plane handles a lot better than my Lockheed Electra did."

If she thought it was a thrill, how do you think I felt? I'm flying through the Bermuda Triangle with Amelia Earhart in 2015 and I can never tell a soul.

I'm definitely going to write a song about this.

When she finished testing the plane, I didn't have to tell her how to get back on track. She turned the plane toward Marathon and leveled it out.

I filled her in on all the events at Rumora and about our plan to poison the Tate fields.

"That just might work. And if it does, I think we should go to Hondue and poison theirs too," she said.

"Good idea."

We arrived at Marathon around two o'clock in the afternoon. I directed her to Johns dock instead of the seaplane dock. The fewer people that saw her, the better.

She bumped the dock and I jumped out and tied the plane to the tie downs.

As we walked to the house, Amelia stopped to look around. I saw her take a deep breath and smile.

"I didn't think I missed this world, but I do," she said with sadness in her voice.

"If you came to live here, just think how you'd miss Rumora."

"Yes, your right. You are lucky Sunny, you have both."

"I know I'm lucky. I've been told many times. Now you have both. You're lucky too."

"I owe it all to you," she said putting her arms around me and kissing me softly on the lips.

"No Amelia, you owe it all to Rumora and that's why you are here now."

We looked into each-other's eyes for a few seconds. I caught myself thinking, "She was very sexy for one-hundred and thirty."

I blinked and broke her spell. I took a step back.

She laughed and said, "Don't worry Sunny; I'm just experiencing feelings that have been dormant for a long time. It's different here than it is on Rumora. It's more real I guess."

"You're right. I feel the same way when I'm there. I can't tell what's real and what's fantasy."

"I guess we had better get in the house," she said.

"Yeah, I guess so."

We entered the house and were surprised at the condition of it. The furniture was out of place and some of it was overturned. There was blood on the floor and some on the walls.

"What the hell happened here?" I said.

"I guess it wasn't like this when you left," she said, looking around the house at the mess.

"No, nothing was out of place."

I heard a siren blasting in the distance. It was getting closer. When I heard it turn onto Johns street I knew there was going to be trouble.

"Amelia, get out of here. Go down by the beach and hide. Don't come back until they're gone."

She slipped out the back door and ran to the plane. She threw her jacket inside and ran toward the beach. I heard a knock on the front door.

I opened the door to find Chief Burk standing there.

"I should have known you'd be here," he said dryly.

"Hello Chief, what can I do for you?"

"I need to talk to John and Rose."

"They aren't here right now. Can I take a message?"

"I received a call saying there was a disturbance here a few hours ago. A neighbor thought they had better have me check it out. The air traffic control picked up on the call and reported John's plane landing here."

"Yes, I just flew in."

"I didn't know you could fly."

"I had a pilot, but he left."

"May I come in?"

"I don't know, do you have a warrant?"

"Do I need one?"

"I guess not," I said and stepped aside for him to enter.

"What the hell happened here?"

"My words exactly."

Chief Burk walked around the house carefully, making sure not to step in any blood.

"Come outside with me Sunny," he ordered.

We went outside and the Chief got on the phone and called for CSI.

"I'm handling this as a crime scene. You're going to have to come with me and answer some questions."

"But I just got here. I don't know anything."

"Get in the car," he said and opened the door.

I had no choice but to get in. Once inside Chief Burk didn't start the engine.

"We'll wait here for the CSI. Meantime you can tell me what you know."

"I don't know anything."

"Where are Rose and John?"

Uh-Oh. I was hoping this wouldn't come up. I can't tell him they're on Rumora in another dimension and being held prisoner by Terrainiens, without sounding crazy.

"I honestly don't know where they are."

"What were you doing in their house and why were you using Curt's plane?"

"He loaned it to me to go to the Bahamas. I just brought it back and I was going to leave the keys in John's house."

"Where did you stay in the Bahamas?" he asked suspiciously.

"I didn't stay. It was just a day visit."

The CSI car drove into the driveway and three men got out. Chief Burk got out and told me to wait here. He walked them into the house.

I couldn't stay around here all day answering questions, so I got out of the car and walked to the beach. Amelia saw me right away and called to me.

"What's going on there," she asked.

"I don't know, but I think I'll be in a lot of trouble if they catch me."

"What are we going to do?"

"We'll hide out the best we can until they leave and then get Bloodshot out of the garage and go get the poison."

"Who's Bloodshot?"

"He's a friend. You'll like him."

There was a schooner anchored at the far end of the beach. It looked like the owners were gone. It might give us enough cover for now.

We walked to the end of the beach, pretending to be tourist. When no one was around so we waded to the schooner and climbed aboard.

The cabin was locked, but the wood was weak. It had been neglected. I kicked the door and it flew open. We ducked inside and sat down. I could see out the windows to the intersection at John's street. I could also see the plane from here.

We sat there waiting, but instead of people leaving John's house, more officers kept showing up. What in the world could have happened there?

A man in a suit walked to the plane and looked inside. He waved at another officer. When he got there they spoke briefly. The first man left and the uniformed officer stood guard over the plane. Soon a lady with a tray walked to the plane and opened the door. She took something from the tray and reached into the plane.

"It looks like their taking a sample of something from the plane," I told Amelia.

Two hours later, they all left. It was five o'clock now and wouldn't be dark for three more hours.

"Let's walk the beach back to the house and see what's in the plane."

"Okay," Amelia said.

We stayed close to the water just in case we had to go in to hide.

When we got to John's dock, we climbed up and looked into the plane. There was blood on the yoke and the seats.

"Oh crap, what's all that?" I said.

"That blood wasn't there when we landed," Amelia said confused.

"This isn't good. Someone is setting us up."

"We have to get out of here. We can land somewhere else and get the poison," she suggested.

"As soon as we take off they will have us on radar. Let's get Bloodshot out and go to the store. It's only two miles up the road."

We went through the house to the garage. The house had notes everywhere and crime scene tape across the doors.

Bloodshot was still where I left him. I got in and started him up.

"Wow, nice truck. Is it brand new?"

I couldn't help but to laugh.

"No, it's probably the oldest truck on the island. It's just in good shape."

I saw her looking at Rose's Bentley.

"That's brand new," I said. "Over a hundred thousand.'

"Dollars?" she said, her eyebrows lifting.

"Yep."

"Damn."

We pulled out of the garage and drove the two miles to the hardware store at the end of the street.

We went in and bought five gallons of concentrated nonselective herbicide.

"This will kill anything that grows and the soil won't be any good for two months," I told her.

While I was in the checkout line Amelia walked around the store looking at all the new products. She hasn't seen anything new since 1937. She picked up everything and read it.

I paid for my herbicide and took it to Bloodshot. I was going to come back in and get Amelia.

I was putting the can in the back when three police cars pulled into the parking lot and surrounded me. They got out with their guns drawn.

Chief Burk walked up to me and told me to turn around and put my hands on the truck. He made a quick search and then handcuffed me. "Sunny, you're under arrest for the murder of John and Rosanna James."

Chapter 27

Amelia stood at the window of the hardware store watching all the commotion. She was going to have to save Sunny, but she didn't have the slightest idea how.

They fingerprinted me and placed me in a cell. There were two other men in the holding cell with me. One, I could tell by the way he was looking at me and flexing his muscles, was going to be trouble. I'm not without my own skills at fighting, but I still hoped it didn't come to that.

Finally he walked over and stood about five inches from me and stared me in the eyes. He made a few little faces like a tough guy and grinned a grin showing both of his teeth. I waited. I knew he would eventually say something and that is when I needed to react, he would be busy trying to say the right thing to scare me.

When he decided the time was right he opened his mouth to talk. I head butted him right on the nose. He fell back grabbing his face and I hit him hard in the stomach. He went down and squirmed on the floor. I walked over to the bench and sat down. My job was done and I knew he wouldn't be bothering me again.

Chief Burk walked in a few minutes later. He looked at the man, who was still lying on the floor, and then at me. He shook his head slightly and asked me to come with him.

"Okay Sunny, start talking," he said after he seated me in an interrogation room.

"About what?"

"About why you killed John and Rose."

"I didn't kill them."

"Their blood was found in the airplane that you just got out of."

"It wasn't there when I got out."

"I found you in their house and there was blood everywhere."

"I don't know how that happened."

"What did you do with the bodies?"

"I never saw any bodies. And if you don't even have any bodies, how do you know their dead?"

"I have a gut feeling."

"You can't arrest me on a gut feeling. I need a phone call. I'm finished talking until I get a lawyer."

Chief Burk led me to a phone and told me to make it quick. I called Thomas Right, John's attorney. I hoped he would help me. He was the only one I knew.

"Thomas, this is Sunny Ray."

"Sunny, good to hear from you again. What's up?"

"I'm in jail and I need your help. Chief Burk has just arrested me for the murders of Rose and John."

Silence on the other end.

"Don't worry Thomas, they're not dead, but it is complicated."

"I'll be right there."

Amelia walked the two miles back to John's house. No one was around so she let herself in. She searched the house for a clue of what might have happened here. It just didn't make any sense.

The house was spotless except for the chairs turned over and the blood. Then she noticed a couple of strands of long black hair on the floor. She picked them up and smelled them. Honeysuckle.

Just like the hair on Rumora. Someone from Rumora was here and set Sunny up for murder. Probably the Terrainiens. They didn't want Sunny to return.

She went to the garage and looked in both cars for keys. None in the Bentley but the Mercedes keys were in the ignition.

She tried to raise the garage door by hand and then remembered Sunny had done it from the car. She got in the car and looked up where she thought Sunny had reached. There were three buttons there. She pushed one and the garage door next to hers opened. She pushed the one left of it and hers opened.

♫

Thomas entered my cell and waited for the guard to leave before he said anything.

"What's this all about?" he said, clearly puzzled.

"John and Rose are on an island. They don't want anyone to know where the island is. I swore not to tell. If I can get out of here I can go get them."

"I looked at the arrest record. They had no business arresting you in the first place. There is no proof of any murder. I think I can get you out of here tomorrow."

"I have to get out today. It's complicated, but it's a life and death situation."

"I'll see what I can do, but I can't promise you anything. Don't mention the life-death situation."

We talked a while longer about the case and Thomas left.

A few minutes later Chief Burk came to my cell.

"Sunny, I don't really think you would harm Rose and John. I know how much you care about them, but I had no choice. But, there is one thing bothering me."

"What's that?"

"Where did you get Amelia Earhart's flight jacket and why does it have her original flight plan in the pocket?"

Oh crap, I thought. How am I going to explain this?

Burk could see I was thinking and he looked at me hard right in the eyes.

"Well?" he said in a demanding tone.

What the hell, I thought. He'll just think I'm being a smart ass.

"She is the pilot who flew me here. I guess she left her jacket in the plane."

"This is no time for jokes Sunny. Where did you get it?"

"It belongs to John. He bought it at some kind of aviation sale. You must have read about it in USA Today."

"No, I don't think I did," he said mockingly. "You're not helping yourself any Sunny."

"When can I get out of here?"

"Never, if you don't start cooperating."

A patrolman came to the cell and told Chief Burk I had a visitor, a "Mary Otis." Then Amelia walked into view.

"I'll give the two of you some privacy," the Chief said.

As he walked past Amelia, he stopped and looked at her. I could see he was noticing the resemblance.

"I told you Amelia was the pilot who flew me here," I said.

"Is that right? Are you the one who flew Sunny here?" he said looking at her.

"No sir. I don't know how to fly," she lied.

"Real funny Sunny," he said and left.

After we were alone Amelia asked me what happened. I told her they think I might have murdered John and Rose.

"Well, I went back to the house and found a few long strands of black hair which smelled like honeysuckle."

"Rumora. The Terrainiens?"

"That's what I figure," she said.

"They're setting me up for this."

"That's what it looks like."

"How did you get here?"

"I drove that big black car that was in the garage."

"John's Mercedes?"

"I guess. That thing has a lot of new buttons compared to my old '24 Ford."

"I don't know how I'm going to get out of here," I said.

"Do you have a lawyer?"

"Yeah, I called John's lawyer, Thomas Right. He knows I wouldn't do this."

"Maybe I could tie a rope to the cell window and pull the bars off with the car."

This made me laugh. God, you just have to love her.

"What's so funny?" she asked.

"I think you've been watching too much of the Keystone Cops."

"Well, it might work."

"Why don't we give Thomas a chance at it first? What did they do with Bloodshot?"

"I don't know. When I drove back past the store he was gone."

"That old guy gets locked up as much as I do."

"You're a bad owner," she said smiling.

"We need that poison in the back of him and we need to get to Rumora right away."

"I'll find a way," Amelia said.

Chapter 28

Chief Burk let me have my billfold so I could give Amelia some money. I told her to go to the Seafarer Inn and get a room.

"Don't try anything. I'll be out soon," I told her.

"Okay, I'll just explore a little."

"There's a cell phone in the glove box of John's car. Keep it with you and I'll call you when I get out."

"Okay. What's a cell phone?" she asked, cocking her head.

I chuckled again. She gave me a look.

"Sorry. It's a telephone that you can talk into and here me. There's no wires, so you can put it in your pocket. When you hear it ring, push the green button, and put it up to your ear."

"Okay."

Amelia left, but I was worried about her out there alone. I sure wouldn't want anything to happen to her.

A few minutes later Chief Burk came in and told me Thomas had arranged a hearing in the judge's chamber in one hour. Thank god for a small town.

The Judge was big man with thick glasses. His name was Howard Pickens. I've him for two years, ever since I opened Rum City Bar. He looked over the top of his glasses at me and then back at the arrest papers.

"Sunny, first of all, I really enjoy your shows on the island," he said smiling.

Good, I thought, he's a fan.

I don't know how you got messed up in this. There really isn't much proof showing that you murdered anyone or that anyone was even murdered, but Chief Burk has a gut feeling. His feelings have been pretty accurate in the past so I'm going to make a compromise. I'm going to place a GPS tracking system on your ankle and confine you to your island for three days. If there is no further proof at that time you are free to go until we get some proof."

"But I really need to leave town. It's important."

"That's the best I can do, and we'll keep it out of the papers. You have a reputation to uphold."

I was being punished for something I didn't do, and worse yet the good people of Rumora were being punished also not to mention John, Rose, Lori, Bonnie and Curt.

"We'll release you tomorrow morning. It's late now and I don't want the Chief out there in the ocean in the middle of the night."

Chief Burk walked me back to the cell and asked if there was anything I needed.

"Well, since you're going to release me tomorrow anyway, can I have my cell phone? I have a lot of people depending on me."

"Yeah, I guess it wouldn't hurt."

Chief Burk returned my belongings.

"Where's Bloodshot?" I asked him.

"He's in the compound."

"Can I at least have the herbicide that's in the back of him? I was going to spray around the island. That'll give me something to do while you prove I'm innocent."

"I guess so."

"And Amelia's jacket. John's trusting me to keep it for him in my safe on the island," I lied.

"I'm sorry I asked if you needed anything."

"Chief, I'm innocent and I can prove it if I can get out of here. Don't worry, you're doing the right thing letting me go."

"You're not free yet. We'll see," he said and left.

I called an old friend, Fast Freddie, who plays guitar at Porkey's to ask him a favor.

"Freddie, it's Sunny."

"Sunny, how's it hangin' man?"

"Loose, how about you," I replied, regressing every time I talked with Freddie.

"Hangin' in there."

"I want you to do me a favor."

"Anything."

"I have a friend I would like for you to meet at John's house and show her where my island is."

"No problem. Should we use the shuttle?"

"No, she's going to fly you there."

"Cool, I hope she's a good pilot."

"She's one of the best in the world. I'll tell you about her someday."

"Alright man, when?"

"Meet her there tomorrow morning around nine."

"You got it."

"Freddie, there's only one problem."

"What's that?"

"I'm going to be leaving with her and there is no boat on the island. You'll have to get a ride home. But don't tell anyone until we're gone. The fans, you know."

"Yeah, I can understand that."

"You can stay as long as you want and use the recording studio."

"You got a deal. I'll see you in the morning."

I hung up and called Amelia. She answered on the fourth ring.

"Hello," she yelled.

"You don't have to yell. Just talk normal."

"Okay,"

"Much better. Can you find your way back to John's house?"

"Sure."

"I want you to be there tomorrow morning. I'll be on my island and I want you to fly there and get me. A friend of mine, Fast Freddie is going to meet you at Johns around nine o'clock and show you the way."

"Good, I'm glad you're getting out of jail."

"Well, when we leave we're going to have to do it quick. The police aren't going to be happy about me leaving the island. They'll probably send a plane after us."

"I guess I get to practice my skills then."

160

"I guess so. I'll see you tomorrow. When we're finished talking push the red button."

"Roger that," she said, "goodbye."

I lay on my cot in the cell and thought about all the trouble I've been in since I left Evansville, Indiana. I've been arrested for murder twice, beaten by some cops, shot at, knocked on the head, a sword fight on griffins, chased by drug lords and now confined to my island. I wondered if this kind of thing happened to everyone under the age of twenty-five. I don't think so. I guess I just have a knack.

To take my mind off my trouble I turned to music like I always have. I started writing a new song. "Amelia"

I was flying one morning-out over the sea
Wind to my back-and feeling free
Thinking how great-my life has been
The world in my heart-like an old lost friend
... ...

I wrote a few more lines and laid my pen down. I was more tired than I thought. The last few days were catching up with me. I fell asleep and dreamed I was flying with Amelia.

Chapter 29

Burk woke me early the next morning.

"You ready cowboy?" he asked.

"Sure," I said, trying to get the fog out of my head.

"We'll stop at McDonalds for breakfast, if that's okay."

"Works for me."

We went through the drive-through at McDonalds and placed our order. I usually try to stay away from fast food, but sometimes you just have to have it. I ordered extra for Amelia and Freddie.

"You expecting company today?" Burk said.

"No, just a little snack for later."

He ferried me out to the island. One of his men placed the GPS on my ankle and sat the herbicide on the dock. "Be careful with that stuff. It'll kill everything," he said.

"Sunny, if you're innocent, I'm really sorry. If you're guilty, I'll get you. Either way I'll see you in three days," Chief Burk said.

No I don't think you will see me in three days. I have a job that needs to get done and I can't wait around here for you to decide rather to let me go or not, I thought.

"See ya'," I said.

I walked to the apartment, fixed myself a good strong Jack Daniels and Coke and sat down on the porch. Just what I needed to get the taste of jail out of my mouth.

I thought back to the last time I was here and Lori was kidnapped and then back to Louie-Louie and Lucy invading my island. It was such a tranquil day before all that happened.

I looked at my watch, eight-thirty. I had about an hour. I finished my Jack, went upstairs and got in the shower.

I never forgot the first time I used this shower. Wanta Mea and Youramine were here for the grand opening and they joined Lori and me in here for an unforgettable shower. I am a lucky man.

Chapter 30

John and Curt worked along the rows of Tate, picking the ripe ones and watering the rest until they were close enough to each other to talk.

"We have to get out of here. The island natives are getting too weak. If they don't get Red Rum or music before long I'm afraid they'll die," John said.

"Yeah, I agree. I know Sunny knows we're here by now. He's probably working on something."

"I wonder what would happen if we started singing?"

"That would make them stronger."

Curt leaned down and pulled another Tate plant from the rich soil. "This stuff grows in a day, but I bet it really eats up the nutrients. I think that's why they have to move from island to island so often."

"Have you seen the girls?"

"I saw Rose under the tent a while ago; She's serving them Rum and Tate. I don't know where Bonnie and Lori went."

John worked his way away from Curt so they wouldn't get busted for talking to one another. When he was a good distance, he started singing Rum City Bar, first softly and then louder. Curt joined in and then they heard Bonnie singing from the other end of the field.

One of the guards took a big drink of rum and yelled, "That's right servants, sing, we like happy workers," and then he laughed.

The other natives looked at each other and started singing low at first too, and then louder. Soon everyone was singing. You could see them getting stronger. The music was working, even if it would be short lived. If they did it every few hours, they would survive until they got out of there.

Fast Freddie pulled in John's driveway at nine o'clock on the dot. He got out of his car and walked around back to the dock.

He saw a young woman walking around the airplane checking odds and ends that he knew nothing about. He could tell she was in good physical shape and attractive, with short sandy hair.

"Hello," he said, "I'm Freddie."

"Fast Freddie, I'm told," she said with a toothy grin, which made her look like a child.

"That's right, and you must be Mary."

"You can call me Amelia."

"Amelia, that's a pretty name to go with a pretty girl."

"Thank you," she said and blushed. She wasn't used to getting complemented on her looks. The only complements she had ever received were on her flying.

Freddie was smitten. He thought she was heart-stopping lovely. And the confidence it took to fly an airplane was more than he possessed.

"I'm supposed to show you where Sunny's island is," he said.

"Yes, I need to take him something."

"Are you dating Sunny now?" he said, and immediately wished he could take it back.

She looked at him for a second, seeing the embarrassment on his face she said, "No we're just good friends."

"Sorry, didn't mean to be so nosey. I guess I just wanted to know if you were available."

"Wow, you work fast," Amelia said, thinking Freddie was quite handsome and glad he was working fast. They didn't have much time.

"Not usually. I don't know why I said that. I think I better quit talking before I say too much."

Amelia laughed and said, "Do you like flying?"

"I did the one time I flew to Georgia and back."

"Well, I'll be gentle."

"Thank you," he said with a slight bow.

They both laughed and Amelia started laughing harder when she heard his infectious laugh.

"I have that effect on everyone," he said.

"That's a good effect to have."

She finished inspecting the plane and climbed in.

"Untie us and push us off," she told him.

He did, almost waiting too long to jump onto the pontoon. He caught himself on the wing support at the last second.

"Man, I almost lost it there."

"Get in before you hurt yourself."

She started the engines and taxied away from the dock area.

"You ready?" she asked.

"I think so."

She pushed the throttles forward and the plane skimmed the water. She eased back on the yoke and lifted it into the air.

"You must really enjoy this," Freddie said, "I don't think I've ever seen such a big grin."

"I've been waiting ninety years to do this again," she said and looked at him.

He knew it was a joke, but the look on her face gave him a funny feeling, as if she was telling the truth.

He didn't laugh; he just looked out the window at the rapidly shrinking landscape.

"See that bridge over there?" he said, pointing at the seven mile bridge.

"Yes, I see it."

"Fly over the center of it and follow those small islands."

She did while looking down at the view.

"It's wonderful here. I have always loved this area," she said.

"Do you come here very often," he said, and thought it sounded like an old pick-up line.

"Every hundred years or so," she said and grinned at him.

He grinned back, but was starting to get uncomfortable. He had noticed her old-fashioned aviator clothing and no make-up and short hair. He thought she looked like Amelia Earhart in the old pictures he had seen of her in the museum. He knew that was impossible, but what if she thought she was Amelia Earhart. Then he was flying with a whack job.

"Over there," he said pointing at an island about four miles away. "That's Rum City."

She circled the island once before landing to make sure there were no hazards to get in her way.

♫

I heard the plane coming and walked down to the dock to help them in. Amelia shut down the engines and let the pontoons bump the dock. I took their rope and tied it off.

"Freddie, thanks for doing this," I said.

"Not a problem. Any time you want me to fly with her, you just call," he said, and smiled at her again.

She blushed again. I noticed the spark between them. Poor Freddie, if you only knew.

"Hi Amelia," I said, and took her hand to help her off the plane.

Freddie stepped over and took her other hand even though it wasn't necessary. Another mutual look passed between them.

"I've got the herbicide and found a sprayer in the storage building," I said.

"Good, we need to get the plane loaded as soon as possible," Amelia said.

"You guys don't need to leave so soon. Why don't we have some lunch and talk for a while," Freddie pleaded.

"We would love to Freddie," Amelia said, "but we have some friends in big trouble and they need our help."

"To bad," Freddie said. "For your friends I mean."

They just stared at each other for a few seconds so I said, "Let's get moving." That broke their stare.

Amelia looked around the island for the first time. "This looks exactly like Rumora?"

"What's Rumora?" Freddie asked.

"It's an island where our friends live," I said.

"Wow, I'd like to see it sometime. I can't imagine another place like this. Are they the one's in trouble?"

"Yeah, they are," I said, hoping to find a way to stop the questions. "Freddie, why don't you show Amelia around the island, while I put the herbicide in the plane. I need to get a few things from the apartment for the trip."

"Sure, I'd be glad to."

Then I remembered the sandwiches. "Are you guy's hungry?"

"Yeah, a little," Freddie said. "I didn't want to eat and then fly."

"I'm hungry too," Amelia said.

I got the bag from McDonalds and gave it to them.

"Cool," Freddie said.

"What's McDonalds?" Amelia asked.

Freddie laughed and then saw she wasn't laughing.

"Really. You don't know what McDonalds is?" he said.

"I don't get out much," she said, and then laughed trying to make Freddie think she was just kidding.

They unwrapped their sandwiches and ate as they walked.

Freddie reached out taking her hand and said, "Watch your step," even though the trail was smooth.

She didn't resist. He led her away telling her how the island was all planned out by John, with his help.

I got my guitar and a small amp and took them to the plane. We needed to spread music around the island as much as possible. Then I had another thought. I have speakers in some of my trees for the concerts here. I also have some left over in the studio. I found the box of speakers and wire and took them to the plane. Then I got my C.D. player and some music and took them also. We were going to blast that island.

I saw Freddie leading Amelia into the studio. They were still holding hands. Good for both of them. I wish they could be together.

When they came back out, I was at the dock trying to arrange everything in the plane. It was crowded, but it fit.

"You have a charming island Sunny," Amelia said, still holding Freddie's hand. "I can't help but think that I've been here before. Is this Church Island?"

I remember John telling me that this island used to be the home of a Baptist church. The locals called it Church Island, but that was ninety-five years ago at least. It was said to have spiritual powers. I know that some people who have visited the island still today have reported a feeling of utopia.

"Yes, it was called Church Island."

"I thought it looked familiar. I visited it several times. I even attended some of the services," Amelia said.

Freddie just stared at her. "How?" he asked.

Amelia smiled her big smile and said, "I'll tell you some day."

Silence followed. Awkward.

I said, "How was breakfast?"

"Strange," Amelia said.

"Sunny, I can't help but notice that you have an ankle bracelet on. What's up?" Freddie asked, changing the subject before he started questioning his sanity.

"I had a little misunderstanding with Chief Burk. He wants me to stay here for three days."

"That's great," Freddie said enthusiastically.

"No, it's not great because I'm leaving now."

"But you'll be arrested," Freddie said, desperate to keep them on the island.

"I know, but its life or death for a lot of people. Please never mention our conversation to anyone."

"What conversation?"

"Thanks."

"Do you want me to come with you and help?"

"It's very dangerous; I couldn't ask you to do that."

"Danger is my middle name."

"That's a nice name, mine is Mary," Amelia said, and then laughed.

"Thanks anyway Freddie. If we need you I'll come back and get you."

Looking at Amelia, he said, "Are you coming back?"

"No, I'm afraid not. I wish I was."

"I'll bring her back again sometime," I promised.

"Good, I can't wait," Freddie said.

"I'll be back in a minute," I said walking to the studio to give them a chance to say good-bye.

I grabbed a few clothes and Amelia's flight jacket and looked out the window to see if I should go back out yet. They were in a close embrace and a deep kiss. I hoped neither one of them would get hurt.

Chapter 31

We finished loading the plane. I took one more look at the island. I was going to miss it. I hoped I was only going to be gone for a short time.

"Freddie, as soon as we take off, the police will be here. You just tell them you didn't know I was in any trouble and I told you I would be back in an hour."

"What should I tell them about Amelia?"

"Well, I guess just tell them she's with me. I don't think they'll ever see her again."

I turned and climbed into the plane and busied myself so they could say one final goodbye.

They hugged and kissed, and said they would see each other again someday.

Amelia reached into her pocket, pulled out the original flight plan from her last flight, and handed it to Freddie.

"Keep this for me, will you?"

"Sure, what is it?"

"It's just an old flight plan that I filed. It was a long time ago, but I think it's probably valuable."

It was valuable indeed. I could imagine the collectors that would love to have that. If Freddie sold it he would never have to work again, but I didn't think he would sell it.

Amelia climbed into the pilot seat and saluted Freddie. He saluted back.

She fired up the engines and Freddie gave us a shove. I watched the light on my ankle bracelet turn from green to red.

I tapped Amelia and pointed at it. "We're on the radar now. Let's go."

She gave it full throttle and we were air born in no time. We turned southeast and climbed to three thousand feet. She turned on the GPS and followed the line to the spot where we had set the GPS from our departure.

Freddie sat on the dock and watched the plane until it was out of sight. He didn't know how he could get that close to girl in that short of a time, but he had.

He unfolded the paper she handed him and looked at it. It looked like an official flight plan. It was typed on an old typewriter. That was odd. He looked at the name at the bottom of the page. Amelia Earhart.

"So far so good," I said too early.

About ten minutes after we departed the radio came alive.

"Marathon calling Cowboys Dreams, come in Sunny."

"Oh shit. I think we've been busted," Amelia said.

"Keep it wide open and just hope we get there before they get to us."

A half an hour into the flight we were surprised by a coast guard plane on our port side. He leveled off next to us and motioned for us to turn around.

"Can we lose them?" I asked.

She just grinned and said, "Hold on."

She picked up her radio mic and said, "Roger that coast guard we're turning around."

She turned to the port instead of starboard and flew right over the top of the coast guard plane. He panicked and dove. Amelia pulled back on the yoke and climbed into the clouds and changed directions again.

The coast guard came on the radio shouting for back up and saying that the pilot was being aggressive.

At five thousand feet, she turned and got back on course.

"Do you think we lost them?" I asked.

"For a few minutes but they'll be back."

They were. Twenty minutes later we were being escorted by two coast guard jets. The radio came alive again.

"Coast Guard nine-five-eight to Cowboy's Dreams, come in please."

Amelia looked at me. I felt sick at my stomach. It looked like we weren't going to make it to Rumora.

"We have to delay them, we're almost there," Amelia said.

She picked up the mic. "This is Cowboy's Dreams go ahead nine-five-eight."

"To whom am I speaking?" they said.

Amelia was quiet for a moment, then she said, "Amelia Earhart."

"Okay Amelia, why don't you just turn that thing around and head back to Marathon, there are a lot of people who have been trying to find you for the past one hundred years."

She looked at me, "Is that true? Are people still looking for me?"

"Yes they are. You are one of the biggest mysteries in the world. People are very curious about what happened to you. You're still loved and admired by millions."

She looked at the GPS, "We're almost there. We can land on the water and they can't. They'll have to get a boat or sea plane out here to get us. By then we'll be gone."

"If you don't turn around immediately we'll have to consider you hostile," came the voice over the radio.

"We're here she said to me."

"Roger that sir we're turning."

She turned, forcing one of the jets to back off. At the same time, she was losing altitude. She did a one-eighty, straightened out and then did another one eighty, all the time losing more altitude.

"What are you doing," the radio said, "increase altitude back to four thousand and turn around."

She ignored the radio and went into a dive. We were coming upon the ocean at an alarming speed. I checked my seat belt and put my hand on the door. When it looked like I should kiss my ass goodbye, she pulled it out, skimmed along the water, and came to a stop.

"Cowboy's Dreams, come in please."

"Go ahead nine-five-eight."

"What the hell are you doing? You know we'll send a boat for you."

"Okay, we'll be right here."

"Lady, what is your name?"

"I told you, Amelia Earhart."

"Okay, but we'll find out who you are, and you will be locked up."

"Will you do me a favor nine five eight?"

"What's that?"

"Tell everyone that I didn't die when my plane went down. I ran out of fuel due to faulty instruments, which took me off course. I live on an island in another dimension now and am very happy."

"Okay Amelia, I'll be sure to do that."

"Thank you."

"You know he was being sarcastic don't you," I said to Amelia.

"Yeah I know, but it's fun to mess with them."

We could hear the Coast Guard calling for a boat.

"I sure hope Paris gets here first," I said.

"He will."

"Look," I said, "The fog."

There it was. The fog that would save us.

"Nine-five-eight to Cowboy's Dreams. There is a deep fog heading right at you. I suggest you turn and take off before it hits you."

"That's our ride nine-five-eight. Tell everyone I love them."

With that we were totally enveloped in the fog. We felt Paris turn the plane and pull us toward the island. We could still hear the radio faintly.

"Nine five eight to base."

"Go ahead nine five eight."

"Cowboy's Dreams was lost in a fog bank. The fog is gone now and so is the plane. They just disappeared."

"We still have a boat on the way to . . . ."

That was it. They were gone and we were in the second dimension again. I felt the plane bump the dock.

Chapter 32

The fog dissipated and we opened the doors onto the island of Rumora. Paris was standing on the dock, soaked from towing us in.

"Amelia, Sunny, I was very worried about you. What took you so long?"

"We had a little run in with the law," I told him. "They think I murdered John and Rose."

"John and Rose are fine, for now. How do they think you could have murdered them?"

"It seems that the Terrainiens have been to their house and set the stage to make it look that way, but I'll clear it up when we return."

I started unloading the gear from the plane. Amelia and Parris picked some of it up and started down the path toward the bar.

"We're going to have to hide this stuff. If they get their hands on it I don't know how we would replace it," I said.

"I have the perfect place," Paris said.

He stopped short of reaching the bar and walked to a large tree. He put his hand on a small branch, which was sticking out on the side of the tree and pushed down and out. The tree opened, and also a part of the open air next to it. It was a door into another world.

"This is where I live," he said, as he walked in and motioned us to follow. "It is close to the dock so I will always be here if someone needs me."

I stepped inside and couldn't believe my eyes. It was very tastefully decorated in modern decor. There was artwork on the walls, which looked awfully familiar to me, but I couldn't name them. I'm not exactly up on all the arts.

Paris set my guitar and amp down in the corner and Amelia unloaded her stash as well.

"Magnificent place," I said.

"Thank you. Wanta Mea and Youramine helped me decorate it. I think they have excellent taste."

"Yes they do."

A door on the right side of the room opened and a very attractive young girl appeared from the bedroom. She was a bit shorter than the rest of the girls on Rumora, but what she lacked in height, she more than made up for in body and beauty. She had the same stunning eyes and nose that Wanta Mea had. Most of the girls here had the same features.

"I would like for you to meet Pleasura," Paris said. "She has been living with me here for the last two weeks. We fell in love at first sight, when she came here from Hondue."

Pleasura walked to Paris, kissed him, and then turned to us. She kissed me and then Amelia. I thought Amelia's kiss lasted a little too long, but they always do.

"Nice to meet you Pleasura," I said. "I've never seen you here before."

"I am from Hondue. I escaped before we were taken over," she said.

"Thank god you got away. Do you know anything that might help us to defeat the Terrainiens?"

"There is nothing we could do. There are too many of them. They take whatever they want, but I think the poison might help to make them week."

"I hope so. It seems to be our only hope right now."

We went back to the plane to get the rest of our gear. Once everything was inside, I asked Paris if he has heard anything new about the people that have been taken prisoner.

"Nothing new. Wanta Mea is down there right now, spying on them. I hope she's being careful not to be spotted."

"Yeah, me too."

"Is this the poison?" Pleasura asked, pointing at the five-gallon container.

"Yes, but I don't know how we're going to spread it. I brought a sprayer, but how am I going to get to the field?"

"I have thought about that. I think Wanta Mea can fly over the fields on her Griffin," Paris said.

"That's a good idea. If she did it at night she might not be spotted."

"I could fly your plane over the fields if that doesn't work," Amelia said.

"Another good idea, but that would make noise and warn them."

The door opened and Wanta Mea entered. "I thought this is where you would be. How did it go?"

I told her the story about me murdering people.

"They will do anything to stop you. I do not like them at all."

"How are Lori and the rest of 'em holding up? Did you see 'em?" I asked her.

"Yes, they are fine, but I don't like to see them locked up like that. They only come out to work in the fields."

"I think we have a plan. Can you get any of your Griffins here?"

"Yes I have Griffins here in the second dimension."

"Great, let's make a plan of action then."

We worked out what seemed to me to be the perfect plan. I was going to warn the servants to stay out of the field tomorrow night. I still don't know how I'll do that, but I'll think of something. Then Wanta Mea is going to fly over the fields and kill the Tate plants. The plants will start to die in two days, but the poison on them will make the Terrainiens sick almost immediately. While they're sick, we can attack them and take the island back.

"Wanta Mea, will the people of the island help us fight?"

"I think they will now. The music is keeping them strong, but the absence of the Red Rum has made them more aggressive. I think they would like to fight the Terrainiens, but they need leadership."

"We'll provide that for them," I said. "We'll even try to arm them with weapons."

"Amelia, I need for you to go back to your people and ask them to play their music as loud as they can. I want to blast music over the whole island. You can take some of these speakers that I brought with me. We'll mount them in the trees as close to the Tate fields as possible and run wires to your amps."

"They'll be glad to. I'll go now and have them start placing the speakers first thing in the morning."

"Tell 'em to be careful not to be spotted. They may be taken prisoner."

"We can protect ourselves. Remember we're strong and don't mind a good fight."

She packed the small speakers in a bag and threw it over her shoulder. "I'll see you at the finish line," she said, and then she kissed us all goodbye.

I hoped I would see her again someday. She was truly a great person.

John had seen Wanta Mea hiding in the jungle. He knew we were working on a plan to get them out of there. He told Curt and Bonnie when he saw them in the field. "When you see Lori and Rose tell them to be ready. I know they're going to do something. We have to be ready."

"I hope it's soon. These people are getting weak, even with the singing. They look strong, but their minds aren't the same. I think they could get vicious," Curt said.

"Maybe that's the edge we need."

Wanta Mea and I walked back to my cabin. It was a beautiful night and it seemed so peaceful, but I knew it wasn't.

"Would you like to stay here with me tonight?" I asked her.

"Yes, I would. I was hoping you would ask me."

We undressed and got in the shower. We held each other tenderly, but didn't make love. I could feel her breath shaking and the tears running down my chest. I wanted to hold her and make all her worries go away forever.

When we got in bed, she melted into me, and that's the way we slept.

181

Chapter 33

"Here's the report you asked for Chief," Officer Daniels said.

"Thanks, did you look at it?" Chief Burk said.

"Yeah, I did, but I wanted to see what you thought before I said anything."

Chief Burk read the report and looked over the pictures that accompanied it. He laid them down on the table and rubbed his eyes.

"Chief?"

Burk closed his eyes.

"Chief, are you okay?"

"I don't know," he said solemnly. "Do you think it's possible?"

"Her Mother's name was Mary Otis, and her middle name is Mary. That's the name she gave us. She looks identical to Amelia and her clothes were the same."

"Yeah, and she can fly a plane like no bodies business. And I wonder where they disappeared to?"

"Did you get a good look at the flight plan she had in her pocket?" Daniels asked.

"Yep, it looked as original as they come. And it matches this one you printed off the internet to a T, except that the paper it was on was old, really old."

Chief Burk got out of his chair, walked out to the front porch and looked at the sky. "Sunny, what have you gotten yourself into now?"

The next morning when I woke, I was still holding her. Our naked bodies felt so right together.

She opened her eyes and smiled at me. "Thank you," is all she said.

I kissed her and the familiar stirring came over me. I wanted to make love to her as I had many times. It was always magical. Instead, I said, "How about some breakfast?"

"The bar is closed, but I think I can find something to eat around here," she said, and slipped under the covers.

Oh well, I tried to take the high road.

A few minutes later we rolled out of bed, took another shower and went to Paris's for breakfast.

He had a spread laid out that would put any Sunday buffet to shame.

"We thought you two might be hungry this morning," he said. "Eat up, we have a lot of work to do."

After breakfast, I started filling the sprayer with the herbicide and water. I had a five-gallon sprayer so Wanta Mea was going to have to come back and get a refill. I premixed the rest of the formula in two five-gallon buckets so we could refill the sprayer fast.

"How are you going to warn the servants to stay out of the field tonight?" Wanta Mea asked me.

"I still don't have the answer to that. I guess I'll figure it out when I get there."

I worked on setting up my amp and placed some speakers in the trees so they would be able to hear the music in the Tate fields. I knew as soon as I started to make music the Terrainiens would come to find us.

"Paris, I want you to stay in your house tonight. They'll never find you there."

"No Sunny, this is my island and I will fight to protect it. I will be by your side."

"We can't let anything happen to you. Without you we can neither enter nor leave the island."

"Yes you can. You have been here enough now that the island knows you and trusts you. All you have to do is land where I told you to and hit your horn. The island will pull you in. You can leave in the same manner. Just stand on the dock and wait."

I didn't know what to say now. I didn't want any of them to get hurt, but we did need all the help we could get.

"Thank you," is all I could say.

We finished the task at hand and went over our plan, what we had of it so far anyway.

"Wanta Mea, you take this sprayer and go to your Griffin. When you hear the music, you will know we are getting ready. Wait until dark, then fly over and spray the fields. Get as low as you can. When the sprayer is empty, fly to the Ora field. I will be in the opening on the south side waiting to refill you."

"Okay, I can do it, don't worry."

"I know you can."

"Just get everyone out of my way."

"I'll figure something out."

"Okay. I love you Sunny," she said, hugging me.

"I love you too, Wanta Mea."

She kissed me and disappeared into the jungle.

"Well Paris, let's see if this thing will make music."

I picked up my guitar and lightly strummed a few notes. The sound was magnified immensely. This was really going to rock the island.

"I won't have long to play before the Terrainiens get here so we'll have to make this quick."

"Not true," Paris said with a smile. "I have a guard."

Paris picked up the mic and said, "Bring in Caspar."

"What is a Caspar?" I asked him in wonderment.

"Caspar is my pet Hydra," Paris said.

The only Hydra I ever heard of was another Mythological creature. It looked like a dragon with eight heads.

The earth shook slightly and a door opened in the jungle in front of us. It was a door in mid-air. The air got waves in it much as Paris's door did. It was partially trees and partially air. This place had so many parallels that I would never be able to figure it out, so I didn't even try anymore. A man came through it leading a Hydra. It looked just like the ones I had studied.

The Hydra saw Paris and quickly moved to his side. It turned and looked at me and bared its fangs.

"No Caspar," Paris said, "Friend."

The Hydra turned his attention away from me and surveyed the perimeter. Paris lovingly petted it and said, "Good boy."

"This is Caspar. He will not let anyone close to the stage or us. The music will be safe."

"I had no doubt the music would be safe, but will I?"

"You will be safe. Come here and pet him. He is a good friend."

I slowly walked to the Hydra. When I got next to him I got a better feel to his size. He was about ten feet tall to his back, and his necks were at least eight feet long. He had six-inch razor like teeth that he would reveal every time his forked tongues would slither out.

I reached up and patted him on the side of his shoulder the way Paris did. One of his heads swung around and looked me in the eye from about two inches away. I felt like I was going to be his lunch. Then he licked me and turned back to sentry duty.

Paris laughed and said, "He likes you already."

"Thank god. I wouldn't want to have to take time for him to make up his mind."

"You can play now," Paris said.

I picked the guitar back up and started playing an old, but lively island song.

The sound was deafening, but it was probably going to do what it was meant to do. The Hydra started pacing back and forth, watching the jungle.

Chapter 34

Curt stood up straight when he heard the music start. He looked at John who was three rows away and smiled. They both new who was playing that song.

He could see Lori and Rose from where he was and could tell they were smiling too. Bonnie came out of the tent, where she was working, and looked toward the jungle.

One of the guards grabbed her by the arm and told her to get back in the tent. She smiled at him and said, "It won't be long now."

He smacked her and pushed her into the tent. Then he returned and nervously looked toward the music.

There was general turmoil of the guards. And then, the leader came out of the tent and ordered for some of his troops to, "Find that music and kill it."

Six of them ran into the jungle toward the music, swords in hand, and ready for battle.

I was playing Rum City Bar now and the trees and plants were growing right before my eyes. Then the jungle exploded with war cries as the Terrainiens ran out of the jungle and toward the stage.

Caspar jumped between me and the onslaught of warriors, who were invading our sanction. They came to a quick stop. A few of them fell down as they were trying to get out of each other's way.

Caspar reached down with one of his heads and picked a Terrainien up off the ground. He screamed and then went silent. The rest tried to retreat to the jungle but Caspar caught three of them before they could. He picked them all up at the same time and silenced their screams as well.

The remaining two fled into the jungle. One ran right into a tree and knocked himself out.

The Hydra let out a fierce roar and flames flew from his mouths. It was his war cry and it was a lot more intimidating than the Terrainiens war cry had been.

Caspar returned to Paris's side and turned toward the jungle again.

"I don't think they'll try that again, do you?" I said to Paris.

"Not if they are smart."

I began playing again where I left off.

The guards, who were laughing when the music stopped, shrank back when they heard the roar and then the music start playing again.

It was Johns turn to smile.

Chapter 35

Amelia was back on her side of the island now. She rang the bell in center of their compound that signaled for the residents to come.

Within five minutes, she was surrounded by famous musicians and friends, who had been fortunate enough to take refuge on Rumora.

One hour later the wires were ran to the speakers in the trees and the stage was set for the concert of a lifetime.

"Listen," Amelia said. "Sunny's playing on the other side of the island and it's starting to get dark. I think it's time for a party."

John Denver picked up his guitar and started the party off with –Thank God I'm A Country Boy.

They were going to play one artist at a time until this was over. The island would be as strong as ever, but without the

Rum, it wouldn't last as long and the peacefulness wouldn't be there.

Right now though, they needed strength and that's what they were going to get.

I looked up at the sky and saw it was getting dark. I knew Wanta Mea would be ready, in about an hour, to spray the fields and I haven't figured out how to keep everyone out of the way.

Then I had a thought. I cranked the amp up even higher and started playing, "The dogs are gon'na bark tonight."

Don't go out in the dark
The dogs are going to bark tonight
Turn you head to the sky and howl

When they hear that lonely sound
 Don't dare come around
The dogs are gon'na bark tonight

There's danger on the rise
The moon will blind your eyes
The dogs are gon'na bark tonight

Stay out of the fields
You'll be safe if you will
The dogs are gon'na to bark tonight

. . . .

I hoped the words to that song would sink in, but if they didn't, I would have to be there to make sure they were safe. Curt heard that song one time when I was writing it.

"Paris, can you play the C.D. player for a while? I think I need to check on the fields."

"Sure can, but I would rather play your guitar if you don't mind."

"Sorry, I didn't know you played."

"Everyone on the island plays."

"Even Wanta Mea?"

"She's one of the best. She plays all instruments."

"Well, I guess I shouldn't be surprised."

"No Sunny, you shouldn't be surprised at anything anymore."

"I guess not."

"Would you like to take Caspar with you to the field?"

"No, I don't think he could sneak up on them. I don't want them to know what we're doing. Besides, I want him here to guard the music."

"We'll still be playing when you return then."

I set off through the jungle toward the Tate field carrying the two five gallon buckets of herbicide. The jungle was much thicker now than it was the last time I came this way. That was good. It was responding to the music.

I noticed some of the thicker areas were parting and allowing me to slip through. The island did know me now and was helping me.

I saw a blood trail leading toward the field. I thought it was probably the last Terrainien that Casper only nicked.

Curt and John were eating their evening meal, which consisted of some kind of soup and some bread. It tasted like old shoe leather, which had been boiled too many times.

"That song," Curt said, "Sunny was just working on it. I don't think it's finished. That's why he cut it off early. I don't think he would have played it for our entertainment. I think it must be a message."

"You think he doesn't want us in the fields tonight?"

"Yeah, that's exactly what I think, because that last line, "stay out of the fields tonight" wasn't part of it."

"Who's on for tonight?"

"I think Lori is," Curt said.

"We need to stop her and her helpers. Any ideas?"

"Maybe."

Chapter 36

I sank to my knees when the Tate field came into view. It seemed empty for right now, but as I watched I saw Lori and three Rumoraians enter the field. This was bad. I guess the message wasn't translated.

I sat the two buckets down and moved closer. I was going to have to warn them to leave even if it meant me getting captured. Then I thought of Wanta Mea. She was counting on me to bring her the rest of the herbicide.

I had about five minutes before she would start. It was dark now and the time had come. If I left right now, I could get the buckets to the Ora field in time.

How could I choose between Wanta Mea and Lori? I had to do so quickly.

Just as I was about to make my move, there was a violent scream, and a Terrainien came running out of the tent on fire. He was beating the flames that were burning his arm and back.

Then another fire rose from the tent where the Terrainiens had their quarters.

One of them ran to the center of the field and yelled, "Everyone to the master tent. Get water. Stop the fire."

The main tent, being about two hundred yards from the Tate field, created the perfect diversion.

I saw Curt run from the tent where the first man caught on fire. Then I saw John near the main tent. I guess they did get the message. They did a good job.

The fields were empty now. Even though Lori ran toward the tent, she didn't help with the fire. She just watched and smiled.

"Good girl Lori," I said to myself.

Everyone was so busy, they didn't see Wanta Mea on her Griffin swoop down on the field and set the sprayer off. It seemed to be working perfectly.

I grabbed the two buckets and ran as fast as I could toward the Ora field. I knew I would only have a couple of minute before Wanta Mea would return.

I was having a hard time running in the jungle with the buckets. As I turned the corner and headed south to our meeting place, I felt a stabbing pain in my right shoulder. I hit the ground hard.

"What have we here," a large man holding a sword, said with a grin. "Where do you think you're going in such a hurry?"

I was in some serious pain. I now realized that this monster of a man had stabbed me.

"What do you have in those buckets? Is that something for me?"

I was having a hard time trying to comprehend the predicament I was in. I looked around for an escape, but there was none. I was trapped.

He raised the sword over his head and said, "Bye-Bye."

As he started to bring it down he vanished before my eyes. Did I see that right? He didn't really vanish he flew away. He was just sucked into the sky. I rolled over and looked up to the direction he had gone.

I saw Wanta Mea on her Griffin and I saw the Terrainien in the paws of the Griffin. He was kicking and flailing. Her Griffin reached down with his beak, and with one swift peck, the Terrainien stopped all movement.

I rolled back over. The pain in my shoulder was intense, but upon inspection, it was just a shallow cut. It could have been worse. Thanks to Wanta Mea, I was still alive at least. Once again, she had saved my life.

I scrambled to my feet and picked up the buckets. The pain was too much. I had to set one bucket down and leave it next to a two hundred foot yellow palm tree. It would be easy enough to find there. I would have to make two trips. I only had a couple of hundred yards to go so it wouldn't be too bad.

I worked my way through the jungle and into the opening where Wanta Mea was waiting.

"Sunny, are you okay?" she cried as she ran to me and threw her arms around me.

"Yeah, just a small cut," I said, looking at my shoulder again. I was losing quite a bit of blood.

Wanta Mea reached into a pouch she had around her waist and pulled out a Toran Root. She rubbed some of the contents on my shoulder and the pain stopped immediately, as did the bleeding.

"You will be fine now," she said, and kissed me long and soft on the lips.

My legs went weak, but we didn't have time for what I was thinking. We needed to finish the task at hand.

I refilled her sprayer and she jumped on the Griffin and took off for another pass over the field.

I turned and ran as fast as I could back to where I had left the bucket next to the palm. I could hear Janis Joplin playing, "Piece of my heart" over the speakers mounted in the trees. From the other direction, I could hear Paris playing a superb rendition of Bob Marley's. This island was in the rock mode and it was responding beautifully.

When I got to the bucket, my heart sank. In my haste, I had knocked it over and it was almost empty. I hoped I hadn't killed this exquisite palm and all the flowers around it. I grabbed up what was left, and ran back to the Ora Field to meet Wanta Mea.

She was just landing from her second pass.

"I'm sorry," I said, "this is all I have left. I must have knocked it over when I was stabbed."

"It will be enough. I will spread it thin and the plants will die eventually."

"Be careful."

"They have not seen me. The fires are still burning. They are busy."

She took off again and I ran back the way I had come. As the jungle spread open for me to make my way through I could hear voices ahead of me. I dove into the underbrush.

They were getting closer and I could tell now that one of the voices was Lori.

As they neared, I could see them. It was Lori and Curt. I stood and called to them. Lori saw me and ran to my open arms.

"Thank god you're okay," Lori said.

"You too," I said. "How'd you get away?"

"It was easy," Curt said, "after I set the fire, everyone was running around like chickens with their heads cut off. I just started walking out. When I saw Lori standing their watching the fire I called to her and she walked out with me. I wish I could have gotten the rest of them out too."

"Thanks for the warning, Sunny. I think I saw Wanta Mea spraying something on the Tate field."

"Yes, we poisoned the Tate so the Terrainiens would get sick and weak."

"Great idea. Where did you get the poison?"

"Marathon."

"How?"

"Amelia Earhart flew me there in your airplane."

"Can this get anymore weird?" Curt said.

"Yeah, a little, I murdered Rose and John while I was there."

"What."

"I'll explain later, we need to get out of here."

"Not me," Curt said. "I'm going back to tell dad and the others what you've done to the fields so they can take precautions. Then we'll be ready when the Terrainiens get sick."

"Are you sure?"

"Yes, I have to. Lori will go with you. It will be awhile before they miss her. I might even set another fire just for good measure."

"Good luck Curt," I said. "We'll get you guys out of there soon."

"Yeah, I know, but what I really want is to make them pay for all the damage they've done to Rumora and the other islands."

"We will."

Curt turned and walked back toward the field. I could still see the fire going and the guards were pretty busy trying to save what little possessions they had.

Too bad they were too lazy to work their own fields. They could probably find a place to live in peace. Now though, they were going to pay.

I put my arms around Lori and kissed her. "I'm glad to have you back."

"I'm glad to be back," Lori said.

"Let's get back to the bar where Paris is, and regroup."

"What's this about you killing John and Rose? And did you say Amelia Earhart flew you to Marathon?"

"Yep, and you're not gon'na believe who her new heart throb is."

"Who? Not you is it?"

"Nope, it's Fast Freddie."

"Oh my god. Now that I think about it though, they would make a nice couple."

"They do."

We stepped out of the jungle and into the opening by the stage where Paris was still playing the guitar and singing.

Lori jumped back and almost fell as she screamed. I had forgotten about Caspar. He stretched two of his necks forward and looked Lori and I right in the eye. He licked me and pulled back. I put my arm around Lori and told her everything was okay.

"Lori, this is Caspar, the protector of music. Caspar this is Lori, my main squeeze." I showed her how to pet him and she did.

He reached down and licked her cheek.

"Wow, that's scary."

"He's a good boy," I told her, and walked past him to Paris.

"We got the fields sprayed and Lori back."

"I see that, I am glad she is safe."

Lori hugged Paris and kissed him.

A couple of minutes later Wanta Mea landed next to us. Lori jumped again.

"Sorry Lori, I didn't mean to scare you. This is my Griffin he is tame and very lovable."

Lori moved forward and petted the Griffin on the shoulder. He turned and pressed his head to her breasts.

"Typical guy," she said.

We need to get all the help we can now and I knew it wasn't going to be easy to convince the people here to enter in battle. I hoped there were enough left in hiding, who were not prisoners.

Chapter 37

As the day passed, we kept the music going. Wanta Mea and I watched the workers in the field picking Tate. The natives looked as though they were smiling now. I guess the word had gotten around about the poison.

The plants didn't look any worse for wear but it had only been fourteen hours since we sprayed it. I knew by tomorrow, they would be drooping some. These plants grew so fast that they should be sucking the herbicide up quickly. I hoped the Terrainiens didn't wash it off too good before they ate it. I wanted the poison to be in their system quickly.

We returned to Rum City Bar and Wanta Mea took her turn playing the guitar and singing. She was good. I don't know why I never knew that before.

Lori and Pleasura were dancing. Lori still had a worried look on her face but Pleasura seemed to be having the time of her life. Oh, to be young and innocent. The two girls seem to have created a bond.

Paris and I sat a table and tried to work out a plan of attack. We still had a few guns, which we knew would be very useful and we had contacted thirty-five Rumoraians, that had not been taken prisoner. They had been hiding in the jungle. They were strong from the music and ready to fight due to the lack of the Red Rum. They were only waiting for our signal.

When Wanta Mea finished her set, Lori took her turn and Wanta Mea sat down with me. Pleasura excused herself and left.

"I think we need to go to the third dimension again to see if the music is working there. Maybe we can get them organized to defend the island from there," Wanta Mea said.

"Good idea, but I don't want to be gone long."

"I do not think there will be a need to be gone long. Everything that happens here will happen there. It is a parallel universe. We are one."

We told Paris and Lori we would be back in an hour or so. They said they would be fine with Caspar to help them.

I held Wanta Mea tight and we were gone. The ride through the tunnel was as sweet as any of the others.

We landed in the same spot as the first time and Wanta Mea's Griffins were there waiting for us.

"How are the people doing here?" Wanta Mea asked the handler.

"They have seemed to get stronger since the music started again."

"Good, we will need them to help us fight. How many Terrainiens are there here in the third?"

"I would say around a hundred. I don't know where they all came from, but I have seen them everywhere. I hide well so they have not seen me. There are probably forty or more prisoners."

The guard watched the young girl, barely clothed, as she walked toward him with a covered tray in her outstretched arms. He smiled at her and slid his sword back into his belt. He was hungry, but the girl would make a much better meal.

He took her arm and pulled her close to him. She kissed him hard on the mouth as she pulled his sword from his belt. She pushed him back and with a mighty force, she beheaded him with one swift pass of his own sword. His head lied on his shoulders for a brief second and the expression on his face was one of puzzlement. Then the head fell onto the floor and the body followed.

She bent down over his dead body and took the key off the chain which had been hanging around his neck, but was now lying on the floor next to the dead body. She walked to the cell and opened the door. "You are free, Tahoe. Your people are waiting for you."

Wanta Mea and I mounted our Griffins and took flight. It was as if this was the first time again.

We flew to the Ora fields to check for guards. They were there. Tahoe had warned us about the land mines that were planted around them, but I guess the Terrainiens still thought they needed to guard them. One was walking across the field and stopped to pick a Red Ora plant. He munched on it as he walked back.

In the distance, I could see two riders on Griffins. They were probably sentries looking for us. I'm sure they knew the minute we arrived. I could tell one was a man and the other was a young girl. They flew away from us as if trying to go undetected. I guess after the last battle, no one wants to fight us again. They disappeared into the fog, which surrounded the mountains that created the valley.

We turned north toward the Tower and the Sovereign One. As we got closer, we could see there was some kind of problem. The guards were in a group at the front door talking and waving their arms.

We landed and one guard and a Centaur came to us. "Tahoe has escaped. They killed a guard and set him free," the Centaur told us.

"How long ago?" I asked.

"Ten minutes."

"Which way did they go?" Wanta Mea asked.

"South," they both said and pointed back the way we had come.

"I saw 'em," I told Wanta Mea. "It was Tahoe and a young girl. When they saw us they turned and flew away."

"Let's catch them," she said, and turned her Griffin and took off.

I was in hot pursuit. I caught Wanta mea and rode beside her. I pointed to where I had last seen them and we adjusted our direction to follow.

Suddenly, we were attacked by four riders. We had to stop pursuit and defend ourselves. It was like swatting flies. They were coming from all directions. I pulled my gun out and shot one in the chest. He fell off his Griffin and plummeted to the ground. His griffin however did not stop his battle. He would fight until he was destroyed too.

My gun was now empty. I should have reloaded it before we came, but I didn't think I would need it. I took a fast look at Wanta Mea who was holding her own against two riders. I would like to help her but I had my hands full.

My Griffin turned over and flew upside down in a quick move to get under the riderless Griffin. I held on tight to keep from falling off. My Griffin struck the other in the soft underbelly and ripped him open. He fell away and was out of commission. The other rider had his sword out, and was coming at me. I made a good move just in time and circled around behind him. Now I was the one pursuing him. He flew in a loop and joined forces with the other two that Wanta Mea was fighting. They all three backed up and hovered beside each other.

I flew to Wanta Mea's side and stopped. "What now," I said to her.

Wanta mea stood up on her griffin and said, "I think I have the strength now."

She raised her arms and brought them down, her fingers pointing at the three men. A flash of light appeared and the three men were blown off their Griffins. The Griffins themselves also flipped and they all fell to the ground motionless.

Wanta Mea sat back down on her Griffin and didn't move.

"Are you okay?" I asked her.

No response. She looked stunned. I moved closer to her and touched her on the arm. That brought her out of her trance. She looked at me with a blank stare. "I am fine. Let's go home."

We flew back to the tunnel slowly. I could tell that the magic really took its toll on her. She was weak again.

The handler took the Griffins from us and led them away. I took Wanta Mea by the arm and forced her to sit down on the ground with me. I sang to her softly for a few minutes and could tell she was getting stronger again.

"Thank you, Sunny. You have made me better again. It seems we just keep saving each other's lives."

"Yes, it does. I wish I could stay here with you forever."

"You can if you want to. It is you who must decide which world to live in. And then there is Lori."

"Yes, there's Lori."

Changing the subject I said, "What are we going to do about Tahoe?"

"We must find him. I know now that he is the force behind all of this. They would not risk their life if he was not important. I hate to say it, but he must die."

Wanta Mea has changed. She would never have killed these men before and now she wanted Tahoe dead. She's a strong woman, but I'd rather have my old Wanta Mea back. I'll make sure she's like her old self before I leave.

"Do you feel strong enough to travel now?" I asked her.

"Yes, I believe I do but first I must get a message to my brother.

She wrote instructions for her brother to be on the watch for Tahoe and to organize the villagers to protect themselves. She gave the note to the Griffin handler.

"Tell him we will be ready for battle by tomorrow."

"I will Wanta Mea. We will be ready also," the handler told her.

I held her tight and we entered the tunnel. The lights in the tunnel seemed to be a different color this time. It was as if it were sensing the distraught emotional state of Wanta Mea. I know I could feel it in her touch. We did not make love but we held each other tight as we did in bed the night before.

Chapter 38

Pleasura was just returning and Paris was getting ready to start singing. I led Wanta Mea to a table and made her sit down. I could tell she was still weak.

"Wanta Mea, are you okay?" Pleasura asked

"Yes, just a little tired."

"We had another fight with four Terrainiens," I told Pleasura. "I think it took a lot out of her."

Paris started the music on the c.d. player, then came and sat with us.

"Wanta Mea, you need to rest," Paris said.

"I'll be fine in a minute."

"Tahoe killed a guard and escaped," I said. "I think Wanta Mea feel's responsible."

"That is nonsense," Paris said. "Tahoe is responsible for his own actions and no one else."

Paris hugged Wanta Mea. "You know I have told you many times, everyone chooses the road they travel. If it turns, you must turn with it or you will lose your way. Tahoe has lost his way because he chose not to turn with the road."

"Thank you Paris, I know you are right."

"Wanta Mea, something I saw back there is bothering me. That guard walked right across the Ora field, picked a Red plant and ate it. He wasn't worried about and traps planted in the field. Do you think Tahoe lied about that so we wouldn't go in the field?"

"That is possible. I think Tahoe would lie about anything."

"That means we could get some plants and make Red Rum. They only poisoned the outside plants so we wouldn't get them and they saved the inner plants for themselves."

We heard a loud noise and turned. The c.d. player was smashed and the amp was gone. The music came to a sudden stop.

I jumped up and ran to the stage. No one was there.

My guitar was smashed like the c.d. player and the amp was lying on the ground behind the stage. The guts were ripped out of it.

I looked at Caspar who was still vigilant and pacing watching the jungle.

"Did you see anyone?" I yelled back to Paris.

"No, you go that way and I'll go this way," he said, pointing in the two directions.

We both took off through the jungle.

A few minutes later, we returned. Neither of us had seen anyone.

"Why didn't Caspar attack when they came for the music?" I asked.

"I don't know," Paris said.

We surveyed the damage. Nothing was salvageable.

Pleasura and Wanta Mea said they didn't see anyone either. "It was as if a ghost came and attacked the music," Wanta Mea said.

"I doubt if it was a ghost. But it might have been someone Caspar knew and trusted," I said. "Is there anyone else around here he wouldn't attack?"

"No, only us," he said, and then, "and Lori, but she is not here. She left before you and Wanta Mea went to the third dimension. She is watching the prisoners at the Tate field."

Thinking about the young girl I saw riding with Tahoe earlier, I got Paris alone and asked him how long he has known Pleasura.

"I met her five years ago when I went to Hondue. When she came to Rumora, to escape the Terrainiens, she came to me for protection."

Paris knew where I was going with this line of questioning. I expected him to defend Pleasura. He didn't.

"Do you think she had something to do with this?" Paris asked.

"Maybe, I don't know, but if she did, she may be in deeper than you think. She looks a lot like the young girl who I saw with Tahoe."

"I hope not, but she was here singing. I care a lot for her, but not as much as I love my island."

We turned and saw Pleasura walking back to Paris's house.

"I saw another thing that I can't figure out. Come with me," I said.

The three of us walked into the jungle in the direction I had taken to look for the intruder. When we came to the spot, I pointed down and said, "What do you make of this?"

There was a six-foot circle of vegetation that was dead. The plants and trees all around it were flourishing.

"What happened here?" Lori asked.

I hadn't seen her join us.

"I'm not sure, but if it's what I think it is, we could be in a lot of trouble," I said.

"What do you think it is?"

"It looks like someone has poured herbicide here. That's about the size five gallons of concentrate would cover."

"Pleasura," Paris said. "She was in my home where we had it stored. I woke in the night and she was gone. When she came in, she said she couldn't sleep and went for a walk. Now I remember she had a funny smell on her clothes."

"If that's the herbicide, what did you spray the fields with?" Lori asked.

We made our way through the jungle to the fields. We could still hear the music playing from the other side of the island. At least that was working in our favor.

We crawled through the last ten feet of jungle and peered through the tall grass. The fields were as green as ever if not more so. I could see John and Bonnie working together. Curt and Rose were not in sight. Other workers were picking Tate also. It looked like they were having a hard time keeping up with it.

"This isn't good," I whispered.

We backed away and regrouped.

"Let's go check on the Ora field," I said.

We walked the path that I had taken to the field to reload Wanta Mea's sprayer. We came to the two hundred foot yellow palm tree, where I had spilt the herbicide. The grass and flowers that I had worried about killing were a good three feet taller than any of the other vegetation.

"Oh shit," I said. "We sprayed fertilizer on those fields. Pleasura must have dumped the herbicide and refilled it with fertilizer."

Chapter 39

John and Curt were noticing the advanced state of the Tate plants the same time we were.

"Something's really wrong here," John said. "These plants look healthier than they did before."

"I'm afraid their plan didn't work. Someone must have tipped the Terrainiens off."

A large guard with an even larger sword walked up behind John and Curt. "Ha! Yes the Tate plants look very healthy, don't they. It is as if someone has been fertilizing them for us. Remind me to thank them when they are here working," he said in a jovial manner. "You do not really think that we do not know everything that goes on do you."

"You know, you won't win this war. When my friends and their friends are finished with you, you'll wish you had never come to Rumora," Curt said.

The guard hit Curt with his fist and knocked him down. "Get to work before I cut your head off peasant."

Curt looked up at the guard and laughed. "This will be fun."

The guard turned and walked away.

"I hope they have a backup plan. We need to get out of here as soon as possible for the sake of the natives," John said. "How's the jaw?"

"Fine, I turned with the blow. It just glanced off."

"I am sorry for bringing Pleasura here. It seems she has made a lot of trouble for us."

"Not your fault Paris. We all choose the roads we travel. Remember?" I said.

"Yes, you are right."

"Let's go check out the Ora field."

Wanta Mea led us to the field. The jungle opened for her and we slipped through unencumbered. The path was vibrant with tropical foliage. Every step brought a new sight and smell from the jungle floor. The music had done its job.

The Ora field came into sight. We hid in the grass again spying on the Terrainiens. We saw Bonnie and Rose in the field. They were walking around the field picking flowers for the rum factory. They were evidently still producing the rum. I noticed they were not using the flowers on the perimeter.

"It looks like the only bad flowers are the ones on the edges. And I don't think the fields are booby-trapped either," I said.

"We must find a way to get some of the rum from the factory. I am sure it is guarded very well," Wanta Mea said.

From here, it looked like there were about five guards in the field. They had swords and were carrying bags, which they were stuffing with Ora flowers.

"One flower will make five gallons of rum," Wanta mea told us. "I hope they are not wasting them."

"How do they know how to make the rum?" I asked.

"My guess is that Tahoe is working in the factory. That was his job and that is probably why they broke him out of prison."

Lori tapped me on the back and pointed to our right. A guard was walking toward us. I don't think he has seen us but he is coming right at us. We all lay down as flat as possible. He was only ten feet away now. He stopped and dropped the bag on the ground and unzipped his pants. He picked the wrong place to relieve himself. When I was sure he was occupied, I jumped up behind him and hit him hard on the head with my still empty gun.

"What are we going to do with him now?" Lori asked.

"I'm gon'na put on his clothes, take his sword, and try to have a look in the factory," I said.

"You will never pass for him with that blond hair," Paris said. "I will do it."

"I hate to say it but you're probably right."

"I will go with you," Wanta Mea said.

"No, you will be spotted too easily. You stay here with Lori and Sunny."

"Better yet, I think Wanta Mea and Lori should go back to the bar and check on things there. Caspar's still there and he'll protect them," I said.

"Good idea. See if you can salvage any sound equipment. There is still my guitar in my home," Paris said.

"Be careful Paris," Wanta Mea said, and her and Lori left, both girls kissing us as they went.

I helped Paris get dressed and handed him the sword and bag. He looked just like one of them. He had been right; I would have never passed for one of them.

We walked through the jungle, around the Ora field and toward the factory. When it was in sight, we stopped. "Just go in and look around quickly. See if they're producing the rum, and how many guards there are. We'll find a way to take the factory back."

I watched as Paris approached the factory. The guard at the entrance didn't give him second look. The door opened and he disappeared inside.

"Good luck," I whispered.

Chapter 40

Paris saw another man empting his bag of flowers into a large barrel. He walked to it when the man left and emptied his. While doing this he took the opportunity to look around. There were three men working in the factory. Paris knew that was all that the factory required. Then he saw Tahoe.

Paris turned so Tahoe would not see him. Tahoe was laughing with Tarek and slapping him on the back as if he had told a funny joke.

So that is how they knew where everyone was, and when to attack. Tarek, the man who was supposed to be protecting us, was working with them.

Paris walked to the door that led to the production area. They were indeed producing rum, red, green, and blue. There were half glasses of the rum on tables. Probably used for taste

214

tests. Paris was sure that the Red Rum was safe from any poisons. Tahoe would not be drinking it if it wasn't.

He walked past a table with a full bottle on it and slipped it into his now empty bag. Not seeing anyone around he also took the opportunity to drink from one of the glasses. The Red Rum ran through his veins immediately sending a flood of utopia to his brain. It felt great. He drank from a Blue Rum and then a Green Rum. He could feel his body reacting to all three. He felt stronger than he had for months. He slipped a bottle of each of the Green and Blue Rum into his bag as well and turned to leave.

Tahoe was standing between him and the door. "Well Paris my friend, what brings you to my factory?"

"This is not your factory. This factory belongs to the people of Rumora."

"Ah yes, but you see the people of Rumora belong to me now."

"Tahoe, do you really think that the Terrainiens are going to let an outsider like yourself be a part of their hierarchy?"

"I am already."

"No you're not. You are merely another of their slaves. They use you to make Rum for them to enjoy. When they are finished, they will kill you."

Tarek entered the room. He was holding a pistol in his hand. "I'll be sure to thank your friend Sunny for the weapon he brought to the island. Pleasura was kind enough to give it to me."

They led Paris out of the building to an open area. Two guards held him and a third blew into a conch shell in three even blasts.

Terrainiens started to appear from the surrounding area and gather in a circle.

Tahoe stood before them and announced, "This is Paris. He is the keeper of the dock. He just tried to steel Rum from our factory. I have decided that he is to receive the death penalty."

I was watching from my spot in the jungle. What was I going to do now? I know that I can't let them kill Paris. I stood and walked to the opening behind Tahoe. "I'm the one you want. Let Paris go and I'll surrender to you," I said.

Everyone turned to face me. Tahoe grinned widely. "Sunny Ray, I was hoping you would show up. I will take great pleasure in killing you. Wanta Mea might be sad for a few days, but she will get over it and then she will come back to me."

"I don't think so, but that isn't any of my concern. Right now I just want you to let Paris go."

"No, I don't think so. I think I will have the both of you killed. It is a wonderful day."

Tahoe pointed at Paris and told Tarek to shoot him in the head. Tarek raised his gun and there was an explosion, but it didn't come from the gun in Tarek's hand. The explosion came from farther away, toward the ocean. Then another explosion went off in the center of the clearing.

The guards were scattering. Some were blown off their feet. They let go of Paris and ran.

Paris came to my side and we backed into the jungle.

"What was that?" he asked.

"I don't know, but . . ." Then there was another explosion from the ocean and another in the field.

"Someone is shooting a cannon from the bay," I said.

Then it dawned on me. Louie-Louie.

"Lucy, give me another cannon ball," Louie yelled.

"Get the hell out of my way before you hurt the wrong people and let me shoot that thing," Lucy said.

216

She stuffed another ball into the cannon and turned the ship two degrees to port and fired again.

Right on target. The Terrainiens were being wiped out five at a time.

Paris and I took the opportunity to charge them and grab swords from the downed soldiers. Swinging them wildly we ran into their disoriented ranks. They didn't have a chance.

John and Curt heard the battle and knew that the time had come. They attacked the guards closest to them and took them down. The other prisoners joined in and like a school of sharks in a feeding frenzy, they wiped out the guards in the Tate and Ora fields.

Paris and I ran back to the bar to join up with Wanta Mea and Lori. Paris handed Wanta Mea the bag and smiled. "You know what to do sister," he said.

She opened the bag and smiled also. She took out the three bottles and placed them on the table. "Are they pure?"

"Yes, they are pure," Paris said.

Wanta Mea drank from each bottle. Her hair seemed to glow and her body stood straighter. She closed her eyes and I could see a wave go through her body. It reminded me of when Popeye ate spinach.

She opened her eyes and asked, "Where are the explosions coming from?"

"Louie-Louie is firing his cannon into the Terrainiens. He's killed many of 'em already," I said.

"Lori, you stay here in Paris's house. We will go and finish this war," Wanta mea said.

"I want to go with you," Lori said.

"No!" Wanta Mea said in a forceful voice. "Sunny will need you later. You will only be in our way out there."

I've never seen Wanta Mea so, so what? So in charge? No, that's not it. So possessed, yeah maybe. It's like she is possessed by a demonic spirit.

"Let's go," she commanded.

We did.

Chapter 41

With Caspar there to protect Lori, she felt safe. She walked to Paris's house and pulled on the branch. The door to another world opened and she entered. Once inside she wished she had followed them to the fields anyway. She knew that being here wasn't going to help her cause any. She started to leave when she heard the door opening. "Great, they came back for me," she thought.

The door swung open and Pleasura entered. Lori knew she was the one who switched the poison for fertilizer.

"What are you doing here?" Lori asked. "If they find you they will imprison you."

"I am here to finish what I started. I will not rest until Rumora is mine and Wanta Mea and Sunny are dead."

"Yours? How do figure Rumora could ever be yours now? They won't allow it."

"You know I am in charge of the Terrainiens? Not Tahoe? Not likely. He is not smart. And the guards, ha! They are idiots, but loyal idiots. They will do as I command. I am their queen," Pleasura said.

"Well Queen, right now it's just you and me, and I still have a score of my own that needs settling," Lori said.

Then two guards walked in the door and stood beside Pleasura. They looked to Lori to be two hundred fifty to three hundred pounds each and had some mighty big swords in their hands.

"You'll never get out of here alive," Lori said, sounding a little worried. "Sunny will hunt you down and kill all of you."

"Oh, you are a little worrier aren't you?" Pleasura said. "Guards, let's go."

The two guards walked to Lori and one took her arm.

"It doesn't look like you're going to settle that score yet, does it?" Pleasura smirked.

"Bring her," Tahoe said as he entered the door. "We will need a hostage. Let's take her with us. Sunny will never let anything happen to her. Once we are safe we can carry out our plan."

Pleasura thought about this for a minute and then said, "Okay, we will take her."

"Caspar!" One of the guards yelled in surprise as they exited the door to find him standing there.

Pleasura laughed, "Caspar loves me. He will not harm us."

Wanta Mea called for her Griffin and they were delivered instantly. Paris, Want Mea and I mounted up and flew toward the fields to find the remaining Terrainiens.

Flying low over the jungle we could see the ex-prisoners running away from the fields. Good, I thought, I'm glad they're free.

Upon a closer look though, I could see that they weren't running away, but that they were chasing the Terrainiens. I've never seen them acting so hostile. I didn't think they had it in them.

We swooped down and joined in the chase. It was turning into a bloody battle. The Rumoraians were definitely getting the better of them.

I flew low over one of the guards and my griffin grabbed him and broke his neck. I saw Paris and Wanta Mea fly into a group of them and start a battle.

Paris was knocked from his griffin and a soldier was beating him with a club. It hurt to watch a good friend getting beat to death. Wanta Mea pointed at the Terrainien soldier and said something and he exploded.

Paris lay limp on the ground. I hoped he was still alive, but I had my doubts. Even in the heat of this battle, I thought how Paris and I had become close friends. It was a sad day.

I should have been paying more attention to what I was doing because the next thing I knew I was lying on the ground. My shoulder felt as if I had been hit by a truck. When I looked up a large guard was standing over me and about to cut me in half with his sword.

"**Let's** go," Pleasura said.

Lori tried to get Pleasura to let her stay but it was no use. She swatted a lamp as she passed it, breaking it as it hit the floor, so Sunny would know that she didn't go peacefully.

They led Lori from the house and took her toward the dock. It was the best exit place from the island.

"CASPAR!" Lori yelled again.

Pleasura laughed. "What a fool you are," she said.

Just then, the two guards that were holding Lori, flew into the air. Lori looked up to see that their heads were completely engulfed in two of Caspar's mouths.

Pleasura and Tahoe jumped back. "We have to go now," Tahoe said.

"Grab her and hold her tight. I'll get us out of here!" Pleasura yelled.

Tahoe grabbed Lori and wrapped his arm around her waist. Pleasura held on to Tahoe and closed her eyes and they all three disappeared.

They appeared on an island in the Bahamas. They were standing on a beach with hundreds of other people.

"Where did we land?" Tahoe asked Pleasura, feeling a little dazed.

"I don't know. We had to leave so fast I didn't have time to navigate."

Lori started to scream and kick at them. People turned and looked, but no one did anything to help her. Pleasura and Tahoe laughed and held onto her as if it was a game they were playing.

"Shut up or I will kill you," Pleasura whispered. "You know we can leave any time we are ready to. They would never be able to catch us."

Lori stopped. She knew Pleasura would kill her. She looked around the beach. People were laughing and playing games, some were drinking colorful drinks and just relaxing in the sun. The smell of sunscreen permeated the air. It reminded Lori of better days.

"Let's go," Pleasura said. "We need to get a room and rest."

"You better rest because if Sunny finds you, you'll be sorry you ever came to Rumora," Lori said impudently.

"Shut up," Tahoe said.

A well-tanned man with long brown hair was watching the trio as they walked away. The two women hanging on his arms asked what was wrong.

"I think I just saw an old friend," he said.

Chapter 42

I rolled to the right just as the sword came down. I could feel the air swish beside my head and I could hear the sword strike the ground. He raised the sword once more for another try. This time I knew I couldn't dodge it. He would be ready. I thought of Wanta Mea and all the good times I would miss if I died right now.

I kicked out at the soldier but missed. He laughed and started his descent with his weapon. I closed my eyes and tightened every muscle in my body, waiting for the end to come.

Nothing happened. I opened my eyes and he was gone. I turned my head and saw Paris on the ground fighting with him. I felt a jubilation run through my body.

I jumped up and secured the soldier in a chokehold, which gave Paris a chance to regain his strength. When he had, he took over. It was like a tag team. Paris was strong now and mad. The soldier didn't have a chance.

The natives were in control now and were gathering the remaining Terrainiens into a group within their circle. This war was over. Rumora would flourish again.

Wanta Mea walked to the edge of the group and raised her arms. Her hair flew wildly around her and the air seemed thick. She chanted once more.

"I call to you who are divine
Protect the island that is mine
Rid our water, sky and sand
Banish these rogues from our land"

A white light engulfed Wanta Mea and rose from her. It moved to the group now cowering in the center of the circle and came down on them. It then flashed blazingly and went away. When we could see again, there were no Terrainiens remaining.

"They are gone forever now. They will never be able to return to Rumora," Wanta Mea said.

There was a cheer from the islanders. They were safe once more and their life would return to normal. I hugged Wanta Mea and she kissed me. "Thank God you're okay," I said.

"Yes, thank God."

Paris came to us and hugged us both. "It is a good day," he said, "but has anyone seen Tahoe?"

"No we haven't. We must find him and make him pay for his crimes," Wanta Mea said.

We mounted our Griffins, which still had a lot of fight left in them, and flew back to the bar. Wanta Mea gave her Griffins their freedom knowing they would come if she called them.

"I'm going to Paris's house to check on Lori," I said.

Just as I was leaving Bonnie, Curt, Rose and John walked into the bar. We all hugged and related a few stories from the last three days.

"I'm just glad that you're all safe," I said.

"Did I hear it right that Amelia Earhart flew you to Marathon?" Rose said.

"That's right. And while we were there I killed you and John."

"Oh, I'm glad I wasn't there for that," she joked.

"Me too."

"What did she think of the way things have changed?"

"Well, the thing she liked the most was Fast Freddie."

We all laughed and I said I had to go get Lori. John and Curt went with Paris and me to his house. When we were inside, we called out to Lori. She didn't answer.

"She was supposed to be here waiting for us," I said.

Lori's bag was on the floor and a lamp was knocked over.

"Something's happened to her," I said. "She wouldn't leave without letting us know."

We searched the island with the help of hundreds of the natives. She wasn't here and neither was Pleasura or Tahoe. Word from the third dimension came to us that she wasn't there either.

"They have taken her with them," Wanta Mea said. "Let me see if I can locate them."

She closed her eyes and chanted softly. When she opened her eyes again she looked sad.

"I cannot find them. The three of them left here together but they did not know where they were going so I cannot pick-up on them. I think they are on an island close by though. They have left the second dimension and are in your world."

226

We all decided that the best thing to do is for the girls to go back to Marathon and John and Curt would take the closest islands north of us and Wanta Mea and I would take the islands south of us. We would stay in touch with our cell phones.

John and Curt left to take Rose and Bonnie to Marathon in the plane. They would drop them off and then search the north islands.

I held tightly to Wanta Mea and we traveled through another tunnel and landed on the small island of San Salvador in the Bahamas.

Chapter 43

"Where are we?" I asked.

"San Salvador, the first stop for Christopher Columbus in 1492," she said adding a little history for my benefit. "This is the Club Med. A very popular tourist spot, but I think this is close to where they landed."

We walked around the pool area and into the hotel looking for any sign of them. The man at the desk looked at me strangely and then approached me.

"Excuse me sir, are you a guest at our resort?" he said in his best English, which was pretty damn good.

"No, I'm looking for some friends of mine, maybe you've seen them. One woman is about five-feet two-inches tall with short black hair. She's with a man with long black hair about six-foot ten- inches tall and a young girl with long black hair about five-feet ten-inches tall. You can't miss 'em."

"I am sorry, you will have to leave sir," he said politely but firmly with a finality that meant no further discussion would be required.

But I wasn't done yet.

"The young lady that I mentioned has been kidnapped and if you're harboring them I'm afraid that your club could be in for a lot of trouble," I said, thinking this would make him see things my way.

He raised his hand and snapped his fingers. Two very large men stepped to his side. Wanta Mea stepped to my side.

"Is there a problem here?" She said.

The men just stared at her. I think they were starting to drool a little. Wanta Mea smiled at them and tossed her hair back away from her breasts, revealing them enough, to make the men forget why they were summoned.

"Do you gentlemen know who this man is?" she asked.

"I told Tony here that I thought he looked like Sunny Ray, the country star," one of the men said, pointing his thumb toward the other.

"That's exactly who he is," she said.

Oh crap, I didn't want that to come out. When people find out who I am, they start singing and want autographs. That's all fine, I love it, but right now I'm too busy for it.

"I am sorry Mr. Sunny Ray. I didn't know," the first man said. "Can we get something for your drinking pleasure?"

"No thank you. I just want to find my friend."

"I think I saw the trio that you mentioned this morning. But I do not know where they went."

"I think they signed in and got a room," one of the giants said.

We looked at the register but of course, there was no Tahoe or Pleasura.

"Do you mind if we just hang around for a while and watch the people? Maybe we will see them," I said, now trying to take advantage of my celebrity status.

"Not at all Sir Sunny. You make yourself at home and we will bring you a big drink with an umbrella in it," the man said smiling widely.

We took a table close to the pool, that allowed us the best view of the area. Two huge drinks were delivered to our table instantly, by a very lovely young island girl. As attractive as she was, she didn't compare to Wanta Mea.

Then we were shadowed by a tall man behind us. "I thought that was you sitting here. When I saw Wanta Mea I knew for sure," the man said.

I turned to see TM. He was one of the drug lords that had caused us so much trouble three years ago. In the end we became good friends when he saved Rose's life. I gave him the account numbers of an account in the Grand Cayman islands that belonged to the crime boss he killed to save her. It turned out that there was about twelve million dollars in that account. I could see that TM has used the money wisely. He now had long hair and was dressed like a very successful man. The last time I saw him his flat top started well back in the center of his head and his clothes were way-too small for him.

I rose to greet him. "TM, how are you?" I said as we shook hands. His grip was firm. I could tell that he had been working out.

"Doing good Sunny," he said and smiled showing his movie star smile. He had had some dental work done as well.

Wanta Mea stood and they hugged.

"You're as beautiful as ever," he said to her.

"Thank you TM. You are looking very well yourself."

"Well, money will do that," he said shyly.

"Do you live around here?" I asked.

"Yes, on the other end of the island. When I saw Lori this morning I knew you would be along soon. It's really good to see you again."

"You saw Lori?"

"Yes, I saw her and two of her friends this morning right here by the pool."

"She was kidnapped by them. We've been trying to find them."

"I wish I would have known that, I could have gotten her back then."

"The people that have her have powers like Wanta Mea. They are from another tribe that invade islands in the other dimensions and take them over. They tried to take over Rumora where Wanta Mea lives, but we stopped them."

"I hope everyone is okay. What about Youramine?" he asked in a panic. He had taken a shining to her not knowing she was leading him on to help me at the time.

"She is well," Wanta Mea said.

TM was then joined by two lovely young ladies, who took his arms, one on each. They gave Wanta Mea the once over with a jealous stare.

They were dressed in very skimpy bikini's, and ripped t-shirts that did little to cover them up.

"Wanta Mea, Sunny, this is April and Heather, my companions. Girls, these are my very good friends, Wanta Mea and Sunny Ray."

The girls perked up at the mention of my name. "Sunny Ray, I thought you looked familiar. Can we have your autograph? Please."

TM laughed, "Sorry Sunny, but you are a celebrity you know."

"That's okay," I said. "I'll be glad to sign one for you."

"I'll be right back," one of the girls said, turned and hurried off.

"I'll help you find Lori," TM said. "It shouldn't be too hard to do. I have a lot of pull here."

"Thanks, we can use all the help we can get."

The girl that ran off returned now with a sharpie for me to sign with. "Here," she said handing it to me.

I looked around for a piece of paper, but there was none. The girl pulled her shirt off over her head and pointed at her boobs. "Sign right here," she said. Then the other girl pulled her shirt off too. "And here," she said.

Wanta Mea giggled and I turned red. I signed in a not very steady hand.

"Thanks," the girls said. "Now when it wears off you'll have to sign it again."

"What about me," Wanta Mea said pulling her skimpy shirt away to expose her breasts.

Being a celebrity does have its perks.

"Okay now let's start looking for Lori," I said. "When did you see her and what were they doing?"

"They were over here by the pool. They were wrestling a little, but laughing. I thought they were just playing, but I guess they were trying to make it look that way," TM said. "They went toward the lobby. Probably to get a room."

"We checked the register but came up empty. Let's spread out and check the resort. Maybe we'll get lucky and find 'em," I said.

We all went in different directions to search. I thought I saw her a hundred times. Every girl here reminded me of her. I could feel the panic in my stomach. I was starting to worry more now. What if I never found her?

I made a full circle and ran into TM again. "Did you see anything?" I asked.

"No Sunny, I'm sorry. I know we'll find her though."

Wanta Mea joined us shortly. "I didn't see them, but some guys over there asked me what I was looking for and I described them. They said they remembered them because the guy and one of the girls were so tall. They said they went in the door at the south end of the building."

"Well at least that's something to go on. We know they're here. I'm going to call Curt and John."

I caught John at his home in Marathon. They were having the plane refueled and the girls were safely home.

"Were on San Salvador, Club Med," I told them.

"We'll be there tonight," John said. "Were bringing some guns."

"Be careful. I wouldn't want you ending up in jail. One problem at a time."

"Don't worry about us. Just find Lori."

We hung up and I went back to the pool area where Wanta Mea was waiting for me.

"TM went to talk to some people. He says he has the connections to find her," she said.

"I hope so. Our window of opportunity is quickly closing."

I looked around the pool area. Young adults were lying around sipping drinks and some were playing volleyball in the pool. There was a lot of laughing and flirting going on. The beat goes on, no matter what kind of trouble you might have.

Chapter 44

"Do you think they'll find us here?" Tahoe asked Pleasura.

"No, I don't think they have any idea where we are. They will find us when I am ready for them too."

"What are we going to do with her," he said pointing to Lori.

"We'll keep her here for a few days and then when we're sure there is no danger we'll just let her go. Meantime though, she is our hostage and our collateral."

"I say we just leave this island and return to Hondue and regroup."

"It is not safe to move in other dimensions right now. Wanta Mea would notice our movement. She is one to be weary of."

"I can't wait to get my hands on her again. She should have never crossed me."

"It sounds like you carry her in your heart still."

"No, I only carry hate for her," Tahoe said.

Lori knew Sunny wouldn't stop searching for her until he found her and that might be his downfall. She wasn't ready for that yet. They couldn't watch her all the time for three days.

"I'm going to go get some fresh air and a drink," Pleasura said. "You keep an eye on her and you can go when I return."

"You don't have to worry about me any longer," Lori said.

"I'll be the judge of that," Pleasura said.

She went out the door before Tahoe could protest. He turned and kicked the bed, and laughed and then cursed.

Once alone Lori smiled at Tahoe. "We're finally alone. Do you want to make love to me?" she said stretching her body out on the bed and rotating her hips.

Tahoe looked at her soft body and beautiful face. He could not stop himself. He went to her.

"Pleasura will be able to sense what we are doing," he whispered.

"I can block her vision. She'll never know."

Tahoe untied Lorie's hands and lay beside her.

Chapter 45

Wanta Mea was the first to see Pleasura at the bar. She had attracted a group of young men that were falling all over themselves to try to get her attention.

"Sunny, look, over there at the bar, it's Pleasura."

I looked. It was her. She was breathtakingly stunning next to the other women and she had quite a crowd around her.

"Let's go get her," I said.

"No, we have to wait until we see Lori before we can let her know we are here."

"Yeah, you're right, but we shouldn't let her out of our sight."

We watched her from the safety of our table, which was blocked by about fifteen men and the bar.

"Oh no," I said, and instinctively grabbed Wanta Mea's arm.

"No don't," she said, when she saw what was happening.

TM and two rather large gentlemen, were walking up behind Pleasura. TM reached out and grabbed her arm.

She turned on her stool and faced him. "Let go of me."

"Where's Lori?" he yelled in her face.

"I don't know any Lori," she said. "Someone help me."

That's all it took. Four men jumped in and freed her then started fighting with TM and his friends.

The battle sent all seven of the men to the floor and fists were flying.

Pleasura took the opportunity to run off. We took off after her. We followed her into the resort and up three flights of stairs. When she got to the third landing, we heard the door open and slam shut.

I eased the door open slowly and peaked down the hall. I could see a door close. That must be the room they are in.

Pleasura just made it in the room before Wanta Mea arrived.

"TAHOE," she said in a panic.

She got no reply. Moving into the bedroom, she walked cautiously. Looking into the room, she saw Tahoe tied to the bed and Lori was gone.

"What have you done Tahoe?" she said, and untied him.

"We have to go in now. They know we're here. They will be gone in a few minutes," I said as I ran toward the door.

Wanta Mea followed me. When we got to the door, I stood back and kicked it hard. The frame gave a little and the second kick forced the door open. We ran inside. Tahoe was standing in the living room but Pleasura was not there.

"They must be in the other room," I said, moving to the bedroom door."

Tahoe blocked my way.

"Move!" I yelled as I took a swing at him.

He was faster than I was and easily dodged my fist. I threw my body into his and he hit me hard in the ribs and then in the jaw.

I had been hit many times but never like this. I went down and didn't know if I would ever get up.

Wanta Mea moved toward Tahoe and he turned his full attention to her. "I'm glad you found me Wanta Mea. I have wanted to pay you back for the last meeting we had in the Sovereign One's castle."

"Well Tahoe, I am here. Move or I will destroy you."

Tahoe raised his hand and a fireball flew at Wanta Mea. She blocked it easily. Then she said with sadness in her voice, "Goodbye Tahoe, I wish things would have been different."

Wanta Mea pointed at Tahoe and what looked like a lightning bolt flew at him and hit him in the chest. He lit up and then vanished.

"He is gone forever now," Wanta Mea said.

I managed to get up off the floor and open the door to the bedroom.

Pleasura was standing there.

She looked at Wanta Mea. "You are stronger than I thought you were. It will be fun watching you die though. I have powers of my own. You will see."

She pointed at me and just as she released a shock meant to kill me Wanta Mea stepped in front of me and blocked it.

"Goodbye bitch," Pleasura said. Then she disappeared.

"Where did she go?" I asked.

"Quiet," Wanta Mea said, and cocked her head as if listening to a distant sound.

A minute later she said, "She is in the Florida Keys. Southern area is as close as I can pinpoint. I cannot tell exactly, when they are in your world. She was wise not to move in our parallel universe. She would not be able to hide from me there."

Chapter 46

John kissed Rose goodbye. "Don't worry about us we'll be fine. The war is over now. All we have to do is find Lori."

"Please find her and don't let anything happen to any of you."

"We'll be fine," he said again.

Curt came out of the bedroom with Bonnie. She'd been crying.

"Are you ready Dad?"

"Yeah, let's get the plane."

Curt picked up the two pistols that were lying on the kitchen table and stuck them in his duffel bag. Rose gave him a sad smile.

"They're only for our protection if we need them," he assured her.

He gave her a hug and then hugged Bonnie again. "I love both of you. I'll see you in couple of days and we'll have Sunny and Lori with us."

Curt and John got in John's car and drove to the airport. They parked in the long-term area and walked to their plane. Curt threw the duffel in the back seat and they started their preflight inspection.

There was a voice from behind them. "John, I knew you weren't dead."

John turned to see Chief Burk standing behind him with two deputies. Burk had his hand on his gun, but kept it holstered.

"Hello Chief," John said. "Sunny told me he killed me a few days ago, but I'm okay now," John said smiling.

"Where in the hell is Sunny?" Burk said.

"I honestly don't know. The last time I talked to him he was in the Bahamas."

"He has a lot of explaining to do and there are some charges against him. He was under house arrest when he and Amelia," Burk waved his hand in the air, "whoever-hart flew away in your plane."

John laughed, "You can say it Chief, - Earhart."

"No I can't say that. People will think I've lost my mind."

"Sunny's fine and we're fine. Someone was trying to make it look like he killed us, and he's after them now. They're bad people, but they're out of your jurisdiction, way out."

"Where did Sunny and Amelia and the plane disappear to when we were watching them?"

"Can't say Chief."

"Can't, or won't?"

"Both really."

Chief Burk looked at John for a long moment and then said, "I'm really glad you and Rose are okay. I know she's okay too because one of the workers here said he saw all four of you get off the plane."

"Thank you Chief."

"But you tell Sunny I want to see him as soon as he gets back. He has some explaining to do, and tell him to bring Amelia whoever with him."

"Sorry Chief, but you'll never see her again. That was a once in a lifetime thing."

Chief Burk swallowed hard and turned red. It sounded to him like John was confirming his worst fear. It really was her.

John's cell phone rang. He looked at the caller I.D. and then looked at Curt.

"Go ahead and answer it John. I know it has to be Sunny," Burk said.

John answered. "Hey Sunny."

"John, Pleasura is somewhere in the southern part of the Keys, but Lori is not with her now. Tahoe is dead and Pleasura knows we're looking for her.

Burk grabbed the phone from Johns hand, "Sunny old friend, this is Chief Burk. How you doing?"

"Sorry Chief. I'll explain it all later. I just don't have time to do it right now."

The phone went dead. Chief Burk handed it back to John and said, "That guy just does whatever he wants to do, doesn't he?"

"Well, pretty much, but right now he is trying to save his girlfriend's life."

"Lori Williams?"

"Yeah. It seems that the same people that tried to set him up have kidnapped her again. They're bad people Chief."

"Yeah, I heard."

"I wish you could help us, but it's really complicated."

"I don't know what you're keeping from me, but I don't know if I want to know. You just tell Sunny I want to see him."

"Yes sir I will."

"Thanks and good luck."

Curt and John returned to their car and called Sunny back.

"Sunny, what do you want to do?"

"We aren't going to do anything. Wanta Mea said she can find her faster without us, and I tend to agree."

"But we have to find Lori," Curt said.

"I know. It's killing me not knowing what happened to her. TM and I are searching the island here. If we find her, I'll call you."

"TM?" John said.

"Yeah, he lives here. He's helping us. We almost had 'em once, but now we're clueless."

"We'll keep an eye out here," John said, "but until Wanta Mea finds Pleasura, we don't have any idea where to look."

"We'll keep in touch. Talk to ya later," I said and hung up.

Sunny and Wanta Mea returned to the pool area. The commotion was over. TM and his two muscle men looked as fresh as they had when they arrived. One man was sitting in a chair and was being attended to by a young woman with a medical bag. Two of the other men were in handcuffs and being escorted away by the local police.

TM walked to where Sunny and Wanta Mea stood watching. "Did you get her?" he asked.

"No she got away. Tahoe is dead though."

"Lori wasn't with them. We need to search the island," I said, already looking around the pool area.

"I'm sorry. I was just so mad that when I saw her I couldn't stop myself from grabbing her."

"We'll find her again and when we do we'll eliminate her," Wanta Mea said.

"Do you know where she went?"

"Southern Keys somewhere."

"I have a plane here you can use, and I'll go with you," TM said.

"Not necessary. Wanta Mea can get there a lot faster."

"I'm still going to help you look for them. I feel responsible now."

"The more the merrier. I'll give you my cell phone number and you can call me if you see them."

We exchanged information.

Wanta Mea kissed me and then kissed TM. "I will find Pleasura and make her tell me where Lori is," she promised.

She then took a step back and vanished.

"Son of a bitch," TM said, looking around for others that might have witnessed what just happened. No one seemed to have noticed.

"Son of a bitch," he repeated.

Chapter 47

Wanta Mea landed in Key West close to Mallory Square. She sensed Pleasura was close by. Her vision was much stronger now, as if nothing was blocking it. She thought of Lori. Could she have been blocking my vision? No, she has no powers. Whatever the reason though, Wanta Mea could now zero in on Pleasura.

As she walked down Front Street, the vibes strengthened. Then she saw Pleasura just ahead of her. She had her now. There would be no escape.

Pleasura was standing in front of a street performer dressed as a Mime. She laughed at his stupid antics and wondered how he would react if she vanished when he came to her with his hat out for a tip.

The Mime approached her and removed his hat. Just as he held it out to her, Wanta Mea appeared and wrapped her arms around Pleasura. The Mime stepped back and took in the beauty of these two gorgeous women hugging. Not unusual for Key West, but when they simply vanished before his eyes he jumped back and fell to the sidewalk.

Wanta Mea and Pleasura traveled through **space** in the second dimension to Rumora. They landed right in the middle of the stage in front of the bar.

Wanta Mea did not let go of her. There was no way she was going to let her escape.

"Take your hands off me you bitch," she shrieked, and tried to break her hold.

"Tell me why you hate me so much," Wanta Mea said.

"No! Just know that I do."

A small crowd began to form around the two girls standing there on the stage.

"Wanta Mea, are you alright?" Paris asked.

"Yes, I'm fine but this little girl won't be if she does not start talking."

"Pleasura, why did you try to take our island? I thought we were helping you," Paris said.

"I used you to come here, because you were so stupid," she spat at him. "I hate you too."

Someone from the crowd yelled to Wanta Mea, "We must lock her up. She is our enemy. If she goes free she will try to take our island again."

"No, she cannot come here unless we bring her here. I have cast a spell on all Terrainiens," Wanta Mea said back to them.

"I am not a damn Terrainien. I was raised on Hondue. I tricked the Terrainiens into making me their queen. They are stupid and cannot resist my beauty."

"Then we will lock you up for the rest of your life."

"Go ahead; it would be better than the life you have already given me."

"I have not given you any kind of life. Everyone is in charge of their own destination," Wanta Mea said.

"Not *me*," Pleasura said with emphasis on, me.

"And why not?"

"Okay, I'll tell you why not."

"No, I'll tell you why not," Reddie, Wanta Mea's mother, said from the front of the crowd.

"Because Wanta Mea, Pleasura is your sister. You two were born three minutes apart. You lived as sisters for eight months. I sent Pleasura to Hondue to live with my good friend Lustie. She raised Pleasura as her own. I would visit her often, but she never knew that I was her real mother."

"But I know now, I found out five years ago when the Terrainiens came to our land. They said they knew a woman that lived here and told one of them of a girl that was being raised to be the new Sovereign One. That she had a twin, although not identical, that was banished to Hondue so all of the training could be focused on her. I never felt like a Hondue native, I always felt different. So, I investigated. I was able to stop the Terrainiens from invading Hondue for four years while I searched for the truth. I told them I would help them take over Rumora if they would follow me."

"So, Pleasura is my sister?" Wanta Mea asked Reddie.

"Yes, she is. I am sorry for not telling you before but I didn't want to jeopardize the training you have been getting. It was very important that you be prepared for the ruler of our country. The Sovereign One, said I had to send one of you away. It broke my heart."

"And mine mother," Pleasura said.

"Yes, I'm sure it did, but I had no choice. At four months Wanta Mea was walking and solving simple problems. She could read at six months. The choice was hard to make but the Sovereign One said I had to keep her here, she was gifted."

"Why couldn't you keep me too and raise me?"

"It is our way. It only happens once every five hundred years and when it does, we have to do what is best for our tribe. In fifteen more years, we were going to invite you back and tell you the whole truth. I am sorry you had to find out on your own."

"You should be sorry. I was raised with no love. As an outsider."

"That is not true Pleasura. You were raised with love. I saw plenty of it when I would visit."

"Yes, that is why I would always look forward to your visits. It seemed I would be special when you were there. I would be the center of attention. But when you would leave, I was just ignored."

"I'm sorry, I didn't know," Reddie said, lowering her head.

Wanta Mea turned to Pleasura, "I am sorry too Pleasura, but how was I supposed to know. I always felt like something was missing but I couldn't put my finger on it."

"That's not all Wanta Mea. You had another sister also. She was sent to live in the first dimension," Pleasura said.

"Is that true mother?" Wanta Mea said turning back to Reddie.

"Yes, I'm afraid it is. I have not seen her since she went away. I know she is living with a good family. Her new mother was from Rumora but chose to live in the first dimension with a man she fell in love with. She asked me to put a spell on her so she would forget Rumora. I did. If I went back to see her she might remember us, and so might my daughter. So I have left them alone," Reddie said, a tear falling down her cheek.

"It doesn't matter anymore. I am an enemy of Rumora now. I could never be trusted to be one of you," Pleasura said.

Wanta Mea turned to Reddie. "Mother, is there anything we can do? Can Pleasura live with us?"

"I don't know how. She is responsible for a lot of pain and suffering on our island."

"But none of our people were killed. Only theirs."

"Pleasura, do you know where Lori is?" Reddie asked.

"I know where she was when I left, but I am not sure now. I told the Terrainiens to kill her if I did not come back."

"Why would you do that? She had nothing to do with all of this."

"Because Sunny Ray was in love with her and I knew it would hurt him," she lied.

"Did you also know that I was in love with Sunny?" Wanta Mea said.

"Yes, I knew that. But I was going to kill Sunny too."

"You have turned into an evil person," Reddie said.

"Yes, I know and I am ashamed of myself. I just went crazy when I found out the truth."

"Is it too late to save Lori?" Wanta Mea asked.

"I don't know. If you let me go I will try to save her."

"I'm not sure that would be safe for my people. You have proved that you cannot be trusted."

"Give me a chance. I will show you that I can. I want to live here with my family now that I have found them."

Reddie hugged Pleasura. "I have always wanted you to know that I am your mother. Now that you do, I cannot save you. Wanta Mea is the ruler of our society. It will be up to her and the council to determine your future. I will stand by their

finding whatever it is, but I will always love you either way."
Reddie hugged Pleasura again then turned and walked away.

"Mother, I love you," Pleasura yelled to her.

Chapter 48

"We will have a trial," Wanta Mea said. "It will be up to our people to determine if you should go free or not"

"Thank you, I will obey the laws. I know they will do the right thing," Pleasura said.

"We will have the trial as soon as possible for Lori's sake."

Pleasura was led to a holding chamber in the jungle. Although the bars were invisible, they were impossible to escape.

"You may have council if you wish. It will have to be someone from Rumora or Hondue," Wanta Mea told Pleasura.

"I have a friend on Hondue. She will help me."

Pleasura gave Wanta Mea her friend's name. Youramine went to Hondue and contacted her. She said she would be there that evening.

The trial was every bit as organized, as any trial in our world's highest court room.

Takeame was the presiding judge as she had been on many other occasions.

The courtroom was entered through another invisible door, which opened into the jungle. The door opened and the counsel and defendant entered with their witnesses and lawyers.

Once everyone was seated, a jury of twelve women entered and took their positions on the side of the courtroom.

The court was called to order by Takeame. The prosecution called their witnesses. The witnesses told how they were held captive by Pleasura and Tahoe. They weren't hurt, but they were made to work in the fields. There were plenty of witnesses with the same claims. There was no proof that Pleasura was the one who killed the guard and freed Tahoe. Although there was speculation.

The defense was given a chance to call witnesses to the stand next.

Pleasura herself took the stand.

"I want to say first that I am sorry for the trouble I have brought to your island. I, in part, am to blame. If I would have been stronger I would not have let Tahoe talk me into helping him. He said if I did what he wanted no one would be hurt and that I would be able to live with my family. It was my dream to do so ever since I found out who they were, but then I got bitter the more I thought about it. I said things that I am ashamed of. I hope you can forgive me," Pleasura said and began to cry. Through her sobs, she looked at Reddi and said, "Please forgive me mother."

Next on the stand was a young girl from Hondue that Wanta Mea knew. Their families were old friends with each other.

"I overheard Pleasura and Tahoe talking one night. Tahoe promised her that no one on Rumora would be hurt in any way. I didn't know what they were talking about, so I kept it to myself. I am sorry now that I didn't tell someone. But I did hear Pleasura ask Tahoe to promise her that no one would be hurt."

Paris sat back and took it all in. He didn't believe a word that Pleasura was saying but he had no proof to dispute her. He wondered how she could fake being in love with him so easily.

After a few other witnesses on both sides, the jury was escorted into a separate room.

They returned in ten minutes.

"We the jury find Pleasura to be innocent of intent to cause any harm to our people or island. We find her guilty of wrongful enslavement. We know how important it is for her to help us to find Lori. We suggest that she be free to find Lori. If she does help to return her to us safely, she should be allowed to live among us. If she does not find her she should be known as an enemy of Rumora and dealt with accordingly."

"Very well," Takeame said. "Pleasura you will lead us to Lori. Once she is safe, you will be one of us. If she is not safe, you will be imprisoned." Takeame tapped the gavel on the desk and the courtroom was adjourned.

Wanta mea hugged her and said, "I am happy to have a sister. Let's go now and find Lori."

"Okay sister, take my hand," Pleasura said.

They held hands and traveled through a tunnel. While in the tunnel, Wanta Mea felt slightly nauseas. That was not a good sign. The tunnel should be a place that only pleasure is felt.

They arrived in Key West on Mallory Square. It was early morning and the area was deserted.

The young girl that testified to hearing Tahoe promise not to harm anyone arrived back on Hondue. A large man was waiting for her there.

"You did well my child. Your family will be set free as I promised. But if you ever tell anyone of this, we will kill all of you."

Chapter 49

Pleasura entered the room. Saturn was sitting on the couch, where he could see her and the door.

"You are back. Was the young lady from Hondue convincing enough?" He asked.

"Yes she was, but I think we should kill her family anyway. I don't want her to tell anyone that we made her lie," Pleasura said and laughed.

"As you wish. That will be a pleasure."

"The stupid bitch is down by the swimming pool now waiting for me to bring her Lori. We will have to leave right away. We still can't travel far in our universe until Wanta Mea is dead. She will detect us right away."

Lori walked into the room from the kitchen. Pleasura was startled.

"Hello Pleasura," Lori said, smiling wickedly.

"So you returned. That was very dangerous. Your stupid sister is waiting by the pool for me to bring you to her. She will know you are here."

"No I have blocked her vision again."

"Don't you want to see your precious sister?"

"Of course I do. I've been waiting for three years to kill her myself; ever since I found out that she and mom dropped me off in this world when I was a baby."

"I don't need you any longer. You are weak," Pleasura said.

"Are you forgetting that I am the one who freed Tahoe? And I also blocked visions and delayed the efforts of Sunny," Lori said.

"A lot of good that did us," Pleasura said hatefully.

"But I am your sister. We were going to rule all the islands together," Lori said.

Pleasura looked at Lori thoughtfully. "Yes, that would have been nice."

"Please," Lori said. "Our mother sent me away to the first dimension when I was a small child. Wanta Mea was ten at the time and mother chose her to be the one child she would keep. At least you were sent to Hondue, where mother could see you occasionally. I never had any contact with her. I was alone."

"But you had good loving parents. I did not," Pleasura said.

"Just give me a chance to seek my revenge," Lori pleaded.

"I'll think about it," Pleasura said softly.

They snuck out of the room and down the steps and away from the pool area.

"If you make a wrong move we will just kill you and disappear. No one will ever catch us," Pleasura said.

Wanta Mea was so happy that she now had a sister and was going to get Lori back. She waited by the pool for another five minutes before trying to pick up the vibes from Pleasura. She could not locate her. Her vision had been blocked again. In a panic, she moved into the second dimension.

She felt Pleasura and another moving away from her through space. It was Lori. The chase was on again as Wanta Mea took-off in their direction.

Wanta Mea was flying through the space created for travel between our world and hers. She was picking up vibrations put off by Pleasura and Lori. They were getting stronger. She was gaining on them.

She could see a faint silhouette starting to take shape only a hundred yards in front of her. She had them now. They would never escape.

Then the shapes were joined by two more shapes and then three more after them. Pleasura was being guarded by the Terrainiens.

They flew toward Wanta Mea, swords in hand. One by one, she struck them down with her powers. They didn't have a chance, but they did slow her down. She had lost sight of Pleasura.

The vibrations sent her off in another direction, but she thought she could still find them.

They broke through the invisible barrier and into their world. Then her vision was blocked again and she lost them.

It was getting late and I was beat from all I had been through. I told TM goodnight, and went to bed. I said we would search the island again tomorrow, but if we didn't have any luck then, we would have to wait for Wanta Mea.

I lay there thinking about Lori. I already missed her. She was the perfect girl for me. We had the same interests and we understood each other's dreams. When we were on Rumora, Lori didn't get mad if I was with Wanta Mea. She often lay with us and shared in our lovemaking. She never had any thoughts about being with another woman in our world, and neither did I. Not serious thoughts anyway.

Now Wanta Mea was Lori's only hope. I prayed she would find them.

Chapter 50

I woke the next morning feeling a little more rested. I lay there for a few seconds before I remembered what had happened. I got dressed and called TM.

"Any word?" I asked him.

He said he was up early and had searched the island again with his men. No luck.

I returned home later that day.

We didn't hear anything that day or the next, or the next week.

I had dates scheduled, performances to play and a tour coming up. I didn't feel like doing any of it.

I had to fill out a police report since I was the last one to be with Lori. They tried to get me to confess to killing her and hiding the body, but they knew better. They didn't try hard.

Wanta Mea had lost Pleasura and Lori. They had managed to get back to the Terrainiens tribe and disappear among them.

Wanta Mea went back to Rumora. There her family and friends were still putting their island back together and trying to get their lives back to normal. The rum was flowing again and the music was playing. Everyone had their strength back and there were big smiles again.

"Mother, what are we going to do about Pleasura?" Wanta Mea asked Reddie.

"There is nothing we can do as long as she stays away from our island," Reddie said.

"I must find her. I have to find out what has happened to Lori. Pleasura is my sister, but she is an evil person. I will not have mercy on her if I find her."

"I would also like to have Lori back. She has been a friend to our island and she was taken away because she tried to help us. I do not wish any harm to come to Pleasura though. She is still my daughter," Reddie said sadly.

"So am I. One of us will not survive this though."

"You come back to me Wanta Mea."

"I will mother."

My concert date was here and this is where the story began. I sat down my guitar and walked back onto the stage for an encore.

"Thank you all very much. I would like to dedicate this song to Lori Williams, the love of my life."

I sang "Lookin' Back." Lori's first number one hit.

Everyone was holding up their lighters and singing along.

When I finished the stadium exploded in applause.

The spot light moved around the floor and lit the crowd. I could see them now better than I did before.

In the third row was a man. He was at least six-foot ten-inches tall and had long black hair. I recognized him. Paris.

I looked around the stadium again following the light. I saw a few others, which I knew from Rumora. Then I saw Wanta Mea working her way toward the stage. She was smiling. My heart jumped a beat. She nodded her head. I went to the edge of the stage and reached for her hand. As I was about to close my hand around hers, her image faded. She wasn't there. She was never there. I just wanted her to be. My heart sank. The crowd got quiet. I stood back up and looked out over them and then everything went dark and I fell.

Chapter 51

Six Weeks Later:

I was sitting in Rum City Bar playing my old guitar, just like I was the day I met Louie-Louie. I haven't played on stage since I passed out. The doctors say I had a lot stress in my system. Wonder what I paid for that diagnoses?

I was still missing Lori and haven't heard from Wanta Mea since I last saw her leave to find Pleasura. I am worried. The two girls I love are missing.

Rose and Bonnie have been spending a lot of time here on the island with me. I don't mind that at all.

I'm feeling strong again and I know what I must do. It's time to go to Rumora.

I played a few more songs on my guitar and then opened a bottle of Cabernet. I held the cork to my nose and took in the aroma of blackberries and grapes. I poured my glass half full and swirled the wine around to catch the oxygen, then I sat it down to let it breathe. Rose showed me how to do that, among other things. When I thought of her, I smiled.

"What ya thinking about?" a voice behind me said.

I turned to see Rose standing there in a very skimpy bikini. I turned red. We were on the island alone today.

"Never mind, I've seen that look before," she said teasingly.

I laughed slightly. She had my number.

"Do you think we could have been happy if we would have stayed together?" I asked her.

"Yes, we would have been very happy, but we're happy now too. At least we will be when we get Lori back."

"I'm going to Rumora."

"I know."

"Want to go?"

"Yes, but I'm not going to."

"Yeah, I thought you'd say that."

"I hope you find her."

"Me too."

Rose sat down and put her arms around me. I felt something stir inside. We sat there not saying anything for a long time. My heart was starting to beat faster and I could feel her breathing heavier. I wanted her bad, real bad, but I would never act on those feelings.

My cell phone rang.

We pulled away from each other not looking any longer but trying to avoid looking.

I pulled my phone out of my pocket. "It's John," I said.

"Hi John, what's up?" I said in what sounded to me like a guilty voice.

"Just checking in on you. How are you feeling?"

Well I was just thinking about how good it would feel to fuck your wife again.

"I'm feeling a lot better. I think I'm going to go to Rumora tomorrow."

"Are you sure?"

"Yeah, I think I better get out of here for a while. I'll feel better if I think I'm doing something to find Lori."

"I'll get the boat ready and I'll go with you," John said.

"I appreciate the ride but I want to go to the island alone. Do you mind?"

"No, not at all, I understand. But I'll still take you."

"Thanks."

"Is Rose around there?"

"Right here," I said, and handed her the phone.

She took it and looked me in the eyes again. I could see sadness in them. Then she brightened.

"Hey sweetie, what's up," she said cheerfully.

I picked up my glass of wine, walked to the bar and took a stool. Rose could still awaken something deep inside of me.

Rose hung up the phone and came to where I was sitting.

"John's coming to get me in a couple of hours. We're going to a party tonight and he wants me to bring you too. You up for it?" she said.

"I don't think so. I think I should rest. I have a big day tomorrow."

"I love you too Sunny," she said, "but we have to keep it under control. We will be friends for the rest of our lives, – unless."

"I know. There won't be an "unless." I'm just feeling down. I just slipped a little there."

"Yeah, me too. That was a close one."

We both laughed. It was a nervous laugh, but at least we laughed.

Chapter 52

The next morning I was up bright and early. John called a few minutes later.

"Missed you last night. The party could have used some entertainment."

"Maybe next time Lori and I will both come."

"Sounds good to me. I'll be there in about an hour. Are you still sure you want to go?"

"I'm ready."

John arrived an hour later with Rose. We loaded my bag on the boat. I left instructions on the table for Fast Freddie to contact John if Lori showed up on the island. I didn't think she would, but I didn't want to take any chances. I knew Fast Freddie would come and use my studio while I was gone.

Before stepping on the boat, I turned and looked at my island. I had a strange feeling I might never see it again. The weathered bar and the wooden stools, with all my friends names carved in them, seemed to be looking back at me and pleading for me to stay. This island was a part of me and I knew I would miss it, but Lori needed me and I was determined to find her.

"Are you ready Sunny? Rose asked.

I turned and stepped onto the boat. I watched the island grow smaller and then disappear as we turned to the open sea.

"**Hi** ya Paris," I said, as I stepped off John's boat and onto the dock.

"Hello Sunny. It is good to see you again. I hope your stay will be a pleasant one."

John and Rose said their goodbye's, and Paris sent them away from the island.

"I will see you when you return to get Sunny," Paris said. "You must stay longer then."

"We will, we promise," Rose said, and waved to us.

We walked to the bar. The path was lush with vegetation much like it was the first time I came to the island. I was glad to see Rumora was back to its old self.

Wanta Mea was waiting for us there. She was dressed in her cargo shorts and a necklace of flowers around her neck. Her long black hair was shining in the sun and her full lips glimmered with a rosy hue. She made my heart skip a beat.

She came to me hugged and kissed me and placed the flowers around my neck, leaving nothing to cover her breasts again. I never want to leave.

"Hello Sunny, I have missed you."

266

"I've missed you too."

"Let's go to your cabin and I will fill you in on Lori."

"Have you found her?"

"No, not yet."

My heart sank again. I was hoping she would be here waiting for me.

There was only one cabin this time waiting for us at the end of the path. We entered and Wanta Mea instantly took off her shorts and turned on the shower. She turned and looked at me. "Come on."

I did as I was told. It was always my favorite thing to do when I arrived here.

We stood in the shower holding each other. I gently washed her and then she washed me. We didn't make love. We just comforted each other. We dried off and had a glass of rum.

Afterward we talked. I told her about my passing out on stage and how I almost made love to Rose. She told me how the island was regaining its strength and the people were happy again.

We finally got around to Lori.

Chapter 53

"**What do you know about Lori?**" I asked Wanta Mea.

"I am sorry Sunny, but I don't know very much. Pleasura got away with her and escaped to the sanctuary of her people. It is impossible for me to get to her unless she leaves their protection."

"Do you think Lori is still alive?"

"Yes, I do. I can feel her. She is still with Pleasura."

"We have to find a way to get Pleasura to come to us. It's our only hope."

"If Lori never comes back, what will you do?"

"I don't understand the question. Do you mean with my life or do you mean, what will I do to find her?"

"With your life."

"I don't know. I'll be heartbroken. I love her very much."

Wanta Mea looked away. There was a pained look on her face, which I had never seen before. Then I understood the question. Wanta Mea wanted to know if I would spend the rest of my life with her.

"Wanta Mea, you know I love you just as much as I do Lori. I would be just as heartbroken if it was you instead of her that was missing."

"I know. I understand. We live in two different worlds. I will just have to be happy to have you while you are in mine."

I took her in my arms and held her. My heart was breaking. I loved her so much, but I can't let Lori go either. I don't know what is wrong with me. Lori, Wanta Mea and Rose. How many more would there be before my life was over.

"I heard that," Wanta Mea said.

"I didn't say anything."

"We were holding each other."

"I forgot, you can read my thoughts while we're touching."

"I will be happy to have you when I can. But now, we must find Lori," Wanta Mea said, wiping the tears from her eyes.

"Do you have a plan?" I asked.

"Maybe. I will have to think about it. It is risky."

"Tell me about it," I said.

When Wanta Mea finished talking, I was in shock. Her plan could bring down Rumora and her if it didn't work. I couldn't let her do that.

"No way; That's too dangerous. We'll find another way."

"We will see," she said dismissively.

Chapter 54

The next morning I woke to find myself alone in the bed. I thought back about the night before. There were feelings coming from within me, which I didn't even know existed.

I got out of bed and ate the breakfast Wanta Mea had left for me. Bacon and eggs, which were still warm and hash browns, a cup of coffee and a glass of orange juice. She must have just left. I missed her already.

I got dressed and went to the bar where everyone gathered for breakfast every morning. A few people were there. Reddie was one of them. I sat down with her and asked her where Wanta Mea was.

"She said she had to go away for a while. She will contact us when she returns. She said to take care of you while she was gone."

"She didn't say where she was going did she."

"No, only that she hoped everything would be settled when she returned."

"Oh, that doesn't sound good. She had some crazy plan to get Lori back," I said.

"I thought as much. Wanta Mea is strong. If anyone can do it, she can. I only hope she can do it without harming Pleasura."

Wanta Mea slipped through the tunnel and turned toward Hondue. This was the last known home for Pleasura and her tribe of land-takers.

She landed in a field about a mile from the main village.

Quietly she made her way toward the village, being careful not to give herself away until the right moment.

The Tate fields came into sight and she stopped to observe. There were fifteen women, by her count, in the field harvesting the Tate.

She didn't see Lori, but she knew she wouldn't. They will still have her somewhere more protected, perhaps in the main house or in the prison. The tall palm trees grew thinner the closer she got to the village. The Terrainiens had cut them down, so no one could use them for cover and invade their village.

Wanta Mea lay flat on the ground and watched the village. It looked like any other village. People were talking and children were playing in the court yards and a young couple was holding hands and making childlike gestures to each other the way young people do when they are courting, but still to bashful to be their true selves. The only thing different is, there was no music and a few of the men had women following them, led by chains, which were fastened to steel collars around their necks. This made Wanta Mea sick and furious. She wanted to shoot a bolt of electricity into the men, but it wasn't time yet.

A few hours passed and darkness came. Now was the time to proceed.

Wanta Mea, keeping low, crept slowly through the darkness and around the remaining palm trees, into the heart of the village.

Staying close to the walls of the grass hut buildings and in the shadows, she made her way to her old friend Toi's house.

She didn't knock on the door but entered quietly. She saw Toi sitting on the floor in the middle of the room. She wasn't doing anything, just sitting there. Toi caught Wanta Mea's movement and looked her way. She rolled her eyes toward the other side of the room and then looked back down.

Wanta Mea lay flat against the wall and slowly edged to the end of it where she could see the entire room.

A big man was sitting in a chair with a bottle of rum. His head was bent forward and he was snoring lightly.

Wanta Mea quietly moved to him, put her finger on the back of his neck, and shot a light volt of electricity into him. She caught him as he fell and propped him back up in the chair.

She looked at Toi and waited for another warning.

"He is the only one here right now," she said. "What are you doing here?"

"I have come to find my friend Lori."

"She is the one from the first dimension?"

"Yes, have you seen her?"

"I saw her a week ago in the village. She was being led by a large man. A Queen's guard, I believe."

"Queen, what Queen?"

"Pleasura has become Queen of the Terrainiens now. She is worshiped by them."

"Do you know how I can find her?"

"Go to the castle. She will be there, but you will never get to her. She is well protected."

"Toi, are you Okay?"

"I am fine, but I don't want to live like this. I wish they would leave," Toi said angrily.

"They will before long, but I'm afraid the land will be ruined from the Tate," Wanta Mea said.

"Our people will starve."

"Will you help me fight them?" Wanta Mea asked.

"What can I do? I am just a weak girl."

"I will teach you."

"Then I will help you. If I don't, I will die anyway."

"Let's go to the castle," Wanta Mea said, pulling Toi from the floor.

Wanta Mea took Toi's hand and led her from her house. They stayed in the shadows and left the village the way Wanta Mea had entered.

"What is your plan?" Toi asked.

"I am going to enter the castle and demand to speak with Pleasura."

"They will kill you."

"I don't think so. Not right away. I am Pleasura's sister."

"Her sister?" Toi asked, astonishment in her voice.

"Yes, I am afraid so. Ironic, isn't it."

"Yes, the one you must kill to save our life and your friends life, is your sister."

Chapter 55

Moving through the palm forest outside the clearing, they walked for a few minutes until they saw the castle. It was a lot like the one the Sovereign One lives in on Rumora.

"Now Toi, you must stay here. When you see me leaving with Pleasura you go back to the village and tell the people to be ready to fight. I am going to try to destroy the remaining Terrainiens that I didn't get on Rumora."

"But we can't fight. We don't know how," Toi said.

"Tell them to use anything they can find for a weapon. If they don't fight, they will die a slow death."

Wanta Mea kissed Toi long on the lips, turned and walked out of the forest toward the castle.

Half way there, she was spotted by the guards. Three of them ran toward her with their swords drawn. Wanta Mea didn't know if she was going to have to destroy them or not. They were being very aggressive.

She held up her hand and yelled to them, "I am Wanta Mea, Pleasura's sister."

The guards stopped the attack and moved more slowly toward her. They have heard of her and her powers.

"Don't worry, I have not come to harm you. I am here to see Pleasura."

"No one sees the Queen unless she calls for them," one of the guards said.

"She will see me. Take me to her."

The guards looked at each other, a puzzled look on their face.

One guard said, "I will go and ask the Queen if she wishes to see you."

Then looking at the other two guards he said, "You stay here and watch her. Don't let her escape."

The guard left. The other two turned toward Wanta Mea and raised their swords across their chests while staring at her.

Wanta Mea jumped toward them and let out a "BOO".

Both men jumped back and one fell over the other's foot and hit the ground.

Wanta Mea laughed and turned to look toward the castle.

Ten minutes later the guard returned with eight other guards. All were armed and ready for battle.

"She will see you, but you must let us tie your hands behind your back," the guard said.

"That is fine with me. I di not come to harm anyone."

She let them bind her wrists, and lead her toward the castle. If her plan didn't work she would probably die here and so would Lori.

They took her to the top floor and knocked on a golden door.

Figures, Wanta Mea thought.

The door opened and four more guards were waiting behind it.

"Are her hands tied?" she heard Pleasura ask.

"Yes your majesty."

"Bring her to me."

Wanta Mea was led into the room where Pleasura was sitting on a throne. Two men were fanning her with palm leaves. She waved them away. They bowed and backed out of the room.

"So, you are a Queen now," Wanta Mea said.

"Yes," Pleasura said in a sultry voice. She sounded a little intoxicated from the wine she was drinking from a golden glass. "What do you want from me? Or did you just come here to die?"

"I came here to join forces with you. I want you to help me to take over Rumora," Wanta Mea said.

"Why would you want me to help you do that? You already rule Rumora."

"Not anymore. They said I am week because I let my sister almost take over the island and kidnap one of our friends. They want me to leave."

"Oh yes, Lori. I guess you came to get her back too."

"No, I don't care what happens to Lori. She is trying to steal the man I love."

"Yes, Sunny Ray. What has become of him?"

"He went back to his world. He is ashamed of me too."

"Lori is still alive. We make her clean the castle every day. She won't last much longer. She is getting weak."

"Good. She deserves to die."

"Yes."

Pleasura raised the gold wine glass and took another drink. It spilled down the front of her covering her scantly covered breasts.

"Guard come here and lick this off of me," she said turning her attention to a young, very muscular, handsome man.

He went to her and knelt before her throne. She leaned forward and he began licking. She moved her breasts back and forth, closed her eyes and let out a faint sigh.

"Enough," she said.

The guard retreated, back to his post by the door.

"Wanta Mea, I don't know what you're trying to do, but you know I can't go to Rumora with my army. You put a spell on them. If they ever return they will die."

"I cast the spell and I can take it off."

"You would do that?"

"I would. We will rule Rumora together, as sisters."

"Sisters, yes, I already tried that once."

"What do you mean?" Wanta Mea asked.

"Never mind. It's not important."

Wanta Mea looked puzzled.

"Interesting," Pleasura said. "And Lori, what will become of her."

"I will be glad to kill her when the time comes. She might come in handy to fool the people on Rumora. Maybe I can use her to lure Sunny back," Wanta Mea lied.

"I will think about it. It would be great, but I don't know if I can trust you."

"You are my sister. That means everything to me," Wanta Mea said.

"What about our mother," Pleasura asked. "Will she join us or will she become our prisoner also?"

"I am afraid she will never turn on her people."

"Well, I have more news for you then," Pleasura said. "I know where your other sister is."

Chapter 56

"You do?" Wanta Mea said, shock on her face.

"I'll tell you someday, when I think I can trust you. But you should know, she would like to kill you too."

"Where is our sister now? Do you know."

"Yes I do. I will tell you when you prove yourself to me."

"You will not be disappointed."

"Guards, feed her and take her to the bedroom next to mine. I will have my decision tomorrow," Pleasura said, and waved her arm to dismiss everyone.

They all turned to leave. "Not you," she said to the guard who had licked the wine from her breasts, "I need you to stay for a while."

Wanta Mea was led to a large dining hall, and seated at a table alone. Food and drinks were brought to her, and set in front of her.

"Would you please untie my hands so I can eat," she said to the guard.

He thought about it for a moment and said, "I better ask the Queen. I don't know if she would approve."

"If you ask her right now she might have your head on a platter. She has a gentleman in the room with her. You know what I mean?" Wanta Mea said with a wink.

"Very well, but don't try anything. I will be watching you," the guard said, and untied the ropes.

"Why don't you join me in some food and wine? I hate to eat alone," Wanta Mea said. She knew how much the Terrainiens loved their liquor.

"Well thank you," he said licking his lips, "I am a little thirsty."

Wanta Mea watched as he drank most of the bottle by himself. She laughed and talked with him to keep him drinking. She let her breasts fall out once in a while and acted embarrassed. He loved it. Finally, she got around to Lori.

"I am going to join forces with Pleasura, your Queen, to take over Rumora. We are going to use the girl from the first dimension to fool them."

"Oh yes, Lori. She is very beautiful. I have slept with her many times," the guard slurred.

Wanta Mea hoped he was just bragging to impress her. Poor Lori if this man did touch her.

"Where is she? Do you know?"

"Yes of course I do. She is down the hall on the left. Her cell is damp and cold," he laughed. "She won't last long."

"I would love to see her," Wanta Mea said, letting her breast fall out again. This time she did not cover them back up. "It would do my heart good to see her that way," she said, and put her hand on her heart and massaged her breasts.

The guard stood and said, "Then come with me. I will show you."

He reached out his hand and Wanta Mea took it. He pulled her close and kissed her. She kissed him back and felt sick. She told herself this is for Lori.

He led her down the hall. It smelled of mold and urine. Water ran across the stone floor in places. She didn't want to imagine where it came from.

They stopped at a wooden door with a small window, which had bars on it.

"Look at her," the guard said, "She is pitiful."

Wanta Mea put her face to the bars. Lori was lying on the cold stone floor. Her clothes were dirty and torn. She looked like possibly the guards did have their way with her.

Lori turned her head toward the door and tried to speak. Her voice was weak and hard to understand, but Wanta Mea could tell she was saying, "water."

"She needs water. I want her to be alive when the time comes."

"She will be alright. We gave her water yesterday," the guard said and laughed. He pulled the canteen from the strap around his neck and poured a little of the water through the window and laughed again.

Wanta Mea couldn't take it any longer. It was not her plan but Lori needed her now.

Wanta Mea pointed at the guard and chanted a small quiet spell. The guard grabbed his throat and fell to his knees.

"What's the matter? Are you thirsty?" she said to the dying guard.

She turned back toward the cell and touched the lock. It glowed and fell off.

Wanta Mea opened the door and went to Lori. She lifted her head and spoke to her quietly.

"Lori, it is me Wanta Mea. I have come to take you home."
Lori looked up at her and smiled.

"Can you walk?" Wanta Mea asked.

Lori nodded her head indicating that she could.

Wanta Mea took the canteen from the guard's neck and gave it to Lori. She drank from it and felt better instantly. She knew she would be safe now.

Wanta Mea promised Toi she would rid the island of Terrainiens, but she must save Lori first. They stood and Wanta Mea put her arms around Lori and told her to hang on.

"We are going to pass through the tunnel and go to Rumora. Sunny is there waiting for you."

"Thank you Wanta Mea," Lori said in a cracked voice.

Wanta Mea closed her eyes and willed them to the tunnel.

"Stop!" They heard as they were fading.

Pleasura had seen them at the last second and grabbed Wanta Mea's leg. She was pulled into the tunnel with them.

The three of them were passing through the void, which spanned the distance between the islands.

Pleasura struck out at Wanta Mea, hitting her hard on the jaw. Wanta Mea fell back loosening her grip on Lori. They started reversing their direction and heading back to Hondue. Wanta Mea held tight to Lori again and kicked at Pleasura knocking her away.

They were going toward Rumora again. Pleasura was still in pursuit. She caught them again and threw more punches at Wanta Mea. Pleasura was a worthy opponent and Wanta Mea was worried that she couldn't fight her and protect Lori at the same time. The tunnel had always been a peaceful and erotic place. This was new to her and she didn't know what to expect. The spirits of the tunnel might kill them both for upsetting the natural balance of its world.

281

Wanta Mea broke away with Lori and made a decision to let her go.

She kissed her and gave her a hard push. "Follow the tunnel and you will be okay. It will take you to Rumora," Lori heard Wanta Mea say in a fading voice.

Wanta Mea turned and faced Pleasura. Then she felt a violent blow to the back of her head and everything went dark.

Chapter 57

I was sitting in my cabin when I heard a commotion outside. I ran out the door to see Paris and Takeame holding Lori by the arms and walking her to me.

I ran to her and put my arms around her. She felt thin and fragile.

"Lori, are you okay?"

"I am now," she said faintly.

I led her to the cabin and asked Takeame to get her some food and water.

I laid her on the bed and covered her face with kisses.

"I love you, I love you, I love you," I said.

"I love you too. Is Wanta Mea here?" Lori asked.

"I don't know. I haven't seen her since she went to get you."

"I think she's in great danger. I lost her in the tunnel. She was fighting Pleasura."

Takeame returned with hot soup and water. She also had a glass of Blue rum. "For the body," she said holding it to Lori's lips.

Lori drank from it and instantly color came to her face.

"That was fast," I said.

"Yes, I feel better already."

"The rum affects you faster than it does me," I said to Lori.

"Thank god."

"Takeame, Lori said she lost Wanta Mea in the tunnel. She was fighting with Pleasura."

"That is not good. The tunnel will be mad," Takeame said with a disturbed look on her face.

"Lori, I was so afraid that I had lost you forever. Did they harm you?"

"Nothing I won't get over. I thought I was going to die. I was scared, more scared than I had ever been in my life. I was kidnapped twice. Why were they after me?" Lori asked, but already knew.

"I don't know. Maybe you were just in the wrong place at the wrong time," I said.

"I want to go home. I don't want to come back to Rumora again. I don't think I could take any more incidents like these."

"I'll get you home, but I must make sure that Wanta Mea is okay. She risked her life for you."

"I know. I'll forever be in her debt. I hope she's alright."

Wanta Mea and Pleasura were spinning through the tunnel. The colors were a dark red now instead of the pastel colors of blue and red that usually accompanied them. A thunderous noise was growing louder and louder.

Wanta Mea was starting to come around again. Pleasura's strength surprised Wanta Mea. She would have to use her powers to protect herself and she didn't want to do that. Pleasura was after all still her sister. Her mother asked her not to harm her.

The tunnel abruptly ended and Pleasura and Wanta Mea fell twenty feet to the ground.

Wanta Mea hit the ground first and then Pleasura landed on top of her, stunning her.

Pleasura rolled off Wanta Mea and got to her feet. She looked around and realized they were on the outskirts of the village.

She yelled for the guards. Finally one appeared.

"What is the matter you majesty?" he asked.

"Tie her hands behind her back quickly. She cannot harm us without her hands," Pleasura ordered.

The guard did as he was told. He tied her hands tightly and then rolled her over.

"What would you like for me to do with her now?" he asked.

"Take her to the center of town and cut her head off. I want everyone to see what we do with enemies of the Queen."

"Yes your majesty."

He led her to the center of town and tied her to a post there. They use the post for whipping prisoners from time to time when they need a little discipline.

Pleasura told him to gather the villagers and then call her. She didn't want to miss the fun.

"**Takeame,** you must gather some friends and help Wanta Mea," I said.

"I will. I can be ready in an hour."

Toi witnessed the guard tying Wanta Mea to the whipping post. She ran through the villages back streets and told everyone she could safely get to, about Wanta Mea's plan to rid their village of the Terrainiens and of her pending demise.

The word spread quickly and the villagers were ready for battle. They knew if it didn't work, they would be punished, or worse.

Toi led a small group armed with shovels and picks back through the shadows of town toward the center.

"We must free Want Mea. If we untie her hands she can help us defeat the Terrainiens," Toi said.

They spread out in order to approach Wanta Mea from all directions. On Toi's command they charged.

They were met by an army of Terrainiens, who easily captured them.

"I told you they would try something like this," Pleasura said. "They are dreamers. Bring Toi here with Wanta Mea. They will both die."

Chapter 58

Takeame returned an hour later with Youramine and Reddie, who were eager to go to Hondue to try to settle this peacefully. They were all ready to do whatever was needed to insure Wanta Mea's safe return.

"We are ready to go. If we can't resolve this peacefully we will make sure Wanta Mea is returned to Rumora safely," Youramine said.

"Please be careful. They are vicious people. They will kill you just for the fun of killing," Lori said.

"We will take care."

The three girls held hands and closed their eyes to enter the tunnel. They disappeared instantly.

"Well, I hope they will be okay. This could be very dangerous," I said.

"I feel like it is all my fault," Lori said.

"It's not your fault. You were kidnapped trying to save their island."

Then we were interrupted by the sudden appearance of the three girls.

"What are you doing back here so fast?" Lori asked.

"The tunnel. It rejected us. It spit us back out. It is very angry because Wanta Mea and Pleasura were fighting in it," Takeame said.

The three girls were very obviously shaken.

"How are we going to help Wanta Mea if we can't get there?" Reddie asked.

"I don't know," Youramine said. "I think I will go by myself once more and try to reason with the tunnel. Maybe I can offer it something."

Youramine closed her eyes and disappeared.

"Well sister, I guess it is time for you to die. Now who is the powerful one?" Pleasura said, and spit on Wanta Mea.

"Why do you hate me so much? I didn't even know of you," Wanta Mea said sadly. "If I had I would have made sure you would be with me on Rumora."

"You say that now, but I know you don't mean it," Pleasura said defiantly.

She turned to the guards and said in a loud voice for all to hear, "OFF WITH THEIR HEADS!"

Youramine appeared before us once more. "I am sorry but I couldn't reason with it. I am afraid we are banished from the tunnel."

We all just looked at one another. We were powerless. If Wanta Mea was captured, we were not going to be able to help her.

"Is there another way to get to Hondue?" I asked.

"There is, but it will take a long time. The Sovereign One will have to help us," Youramine said.

"Let's go talk to her then. We don't have time to waste."

"She will not be very willing to help," Takeame said, "It will cost her."

"Cost her, how?"

"She will have to confess to the other world spirits that one of her people took place in violence. She might be stripped of her throne then maybe they will say Wanta Mea will never be able to replace her. Something has to happen if we bring it to the attention of other worlds."

"Isn't that better than losing Wanta Mea?"

"Not if it is better for the whole."

I was sick. It looked like Wanta Mea was on her own. I couldn't bear the thought of never seeing her again.

Lori took my hand and we walked to Rum City Bar. The music was playing and everyone was singing and dancing. They had no idea the trouble Wanta Mea might be in.

"Maybe Wanta Mea doesn't even need our help," Lori said, trying to console me. "Maybe she is fine. She might be home any minute now."

"Yeah, maybe," I said in a soft voice. I had a bad feeling that we wouldn't be seeing her any time soon. If ever.

"**Wait,**" Wanta Mea yelled. "Is Toi my sister?"

Pleasura laughed, "No, you idiot. Lori is your sister."

Wanta Mea was stunned.

"Lori is the one with powers to block your visions. She was going to rule Rumora with me, but I didn't trust her. I guess I should have. She was the one, which hit you on the head in the tunnel."

"But Lori loves Sunny," Wanta Mea said puzzled.

"Maybe a little. She only met him so he would eventually bring her to Rumora. A very elaborate plan. It almost worked."

"But mother would have known Lori if she was her daughter."

"Lori can change her appearance. She also blocked mother from sensing her. She has very strong powers, but they don't do much good in battle."

Pleasura waved her hand.

The ax started down splitting the air and making a whooshing sound-and there was silence from the crowd of onlookers.

Chapter 59

Lori and I stayed on Rumora for two more weeks. Every day we thought might be the day Wanta Mea returned. It never happened.

We made our plans to leave. Youramine went to John's house and told him of Wanta Mea and that we were ready to come home. Three days later, he was at the dock on Rumora.

There was a ceremony for Wanta Mea on the day John arrived. Rose, Curt and Bonnie were with him. Two days later, we left the island. I don't know if I'll ever be able to return. It just wouldn't be the same.

My next few months were spent in a daze. I was heartsick. Lori said it was time for me to start living my life again as she had. She seemed to have a hard time getting over being kidnapped and I'm afraid I wasn't there for her during her recovery much.

A month later, I had my first concert. My fans were glad to see me return and I did a good job hiding my grief. As time went on, I forced myself to stop thinking about Rumora and Wanta Mea as often.

My old friend and former enemy T.M. came to see me a few times and tried to cheer me up. He had some interesting stories to tell of his adventures of the last few years. At least he wasn't selling drugs anymore.

Things didn't seem the same with Lori any longer. We didn't have that special something, which always kept us so close. I could feel her drifting away, as if she were preoccupied.

One day she came to me and said she was going to have to go away for a while.

"What about your singing and your fans? You can't just turn your back on all of that. There are people depending on you," I said.

"I didn't really want all that stuff anyway," she said. "They'll get over it."

And with that she vanished right before my eyes.

"What the hell?"

Chapter 60

I was sitting at Rum City Bar playing my old guitar. My favorite thing to do anymore. I enjoyed it more than playing for thousands of fans. I think I might be getting burned out.

I decided it was time to return to Rumora to see if they found out what happened to Wanta Mea.

I packed my bag and fueled up my boat. I had my own seventy-five footer now and I could handle it.

I called Fast Freddie and asked him to come to the island and keep an eye on it for me while I was gone. He was only too happy to do it.

Freddie and I were sitting on the dock having a bottle of wine and talking about what we were going to do in the future. He said he wanted to live my life and I said I wanted to live his. Except I wanted to live his life on Rumora.

While we were talking, I looked out over the horizon and noticed a large schooner lazily tacking back and forth and heading for my island.

"What do you make of that?" Freddie asked me.

"I don't know. I wonder where he's going?"

"Nothing out here but us."

"Oh shit. Freddie I think we better get to our feet and get ready to run."

Louie turned the schooner again and filled the sails with a strong wind, which was bringing the ship straight at us.

"If that's who I think it is, we'll be killed if we stay here."

Then I saw the blond hair flying on the bow of the ship. She was holding the rum bottle over her head and leaning back riding the waves.

"RUN FREDDIE!" I yelled.

We did. Just in time. The schooner broke right through the dock and onto the beach just as it did the last time. Palms were knocked down and coconuts were flying.

Then came the familiar, BOOM, from the cannon and the top of my cupola went flying through the air.

Freddie was running looking back at the rapidly approaching ship and ran right into a palm tree. He fell back and was lying in the sand on his back. The ship stopped before it killed either one of us.

"HEY SUNNY," Lucy yelled from the bow, "HOW YOU DOIN'."

I was hiding under the bar and stuck my head out. "Doing okay. How 'bout you?"

"What the hell," Freddie said.

About that time, Louie threw his leg over the side of the ship and fell the twenty feet to the sand. I ran over to help him and see if he was okay.

"Fuckin' ladder," he said, "I gotta' get a new one."

"Hey you stupid fuck," Lucy yelled, "You forgot to throw the ladder over the side."

Lucy threw it over and came down.

She walked to where Freddie was still sitting in the sand. "You Fast Freddie?" she asked.

"Yeah," he answered, still dazed from the tree and wondering why these people just sailed onto the island and why I wasn't yelling at them.

"I got something for you," Lucy said.

She turned to the boat and yelled, "AMELIA!"

Amelia came out of the cabin and waved at Freddie with a big smile on her face.

"Amelia," he said softly, and then louder.

She climbed down the ladder and threw her arms around him.

"How did you know Freddie was going to be on my island?" I asked Lucy.

"We pay attention. We knew you were getting ready to come to Rumora and that Freddie would be watching your island. So we decided to bring her here to keep him company while we took you to Rumora."

Chapter 61

Life on Rumora went on as it had for all the thousands of years before Sunny Ray or Wanta Mea for that matter, had lived there.

Takeame, Youramine and Reddie lived there lives happily. John Denver still came to the bar and played music. All was good.

"Mother, do you think I will ever be able to go see Sunny again?" Wanta Mea asked Reddie.

"I think you will know when the time is right. He is not with Lori anymore and she was the reason you chose not to go to him when you first returned from Hondue."

"I wanted to give them a chance to decide on their own if they were meant to be together, but now Sunny is alone and I want to be with him. I have watched him at his concerts; he seems to be empty of spirit."

"We just got you back and I don't want to see you go again, but I do want you to be happy," Reddie said with a heavy hart only a mother could feel. "You know the Sovereign One said you can't leave the island for a few years while your training is in its final stage. You will see Sunny soon enough."

"Mother I am so sorry you had to lose two of your children for the other to survive. I know you loved Pleasura too. If I could have gotten out of it any other way I would have, but she left me no choice," Wanta Mea said.

"I only wish I would have known that Lori was my other child," Reddie said with sadness in her voice. "Maybe I could have explained to her how it must be and that I had no choice."

Wanta Mea waited until the very last second to use her fingers to burn the ropes, which bound her hands. She thought Pleasura would change her mind, but she didn't. She cast a lightning bolt into the Terrainiens but not at Pleasura. The Terrainiens were all gone now. They were sent in all directions. They had lost their leader now and would probably never be united as a tribe again.

Wanta Mea thought that would be better than killing them. They would have to learn to live in peace with others now to survive.

The villagers took Pleasura after they were free. Wanta Mea could not stop them without harming all of them.

"I am sorry," Wanta Mea said lowering her head. She had told her mother many times and Reddie had always told her she did the right thing, but it was still hard to cause the death of your sister.

Wanta Mea went into the tunnel and begged it not to turn all of the innocent away for her sins. After a month's deliberation, the tunnel decided Wanta Mea was only doing what she had to do to keep peace and save lives. All was forgiven.

"Mother, what about Lori? Will she ever come to Rumora again?"

"I hope so. I had no idea she was actually my daughter. She has the ability to block visions from us. A very strong power.

"**Well** Sunny, you going with us?" Lucy said.

"Of course I am. Let's go."

"Goodbye Amelia. Let us know when you're ready to return and we'll be here in five minutes," Louie said.

"I will. Take your time though."

I climbed the ladder and took my place on the front of the bow next to Lucy. "It sure would be a happier trip if Wanta Mea was waiting for me," I said.

Lucy and Louie exchanged a smile.

The ship backed back across the island and all the trees stood back up as we passed them.

We turned once we were clear of the island and we disappeared into a thick fog bank.

Epilogue

I chose to live my next few years on Rumora. Wanta Mea and I were married in the Ora fields where we had defeated the Terrainiens. I couldn't believe my eyes when I saw her sitting at the bar.

I would return home just enough to stay in the public eye and keep my real life intact.

I knew someday, my real life would have nothing to do with the first dimension.

She explained to me that Lori was her sister and had originally met me hoping to get to Rumora. It worked.

It was hard to believe she used me for three years. I still cherish the time I spent with her. I believe she did love me.

On Hondue, life also went on as it had for thousands of years. Toi was considered a hero, as was Wanta Mea.

Laughter and merriment could be heard from the deep, damp dungeon, which was Pleasura's home.

"I will have my revenge. Wanta Mea and Sunny will be sorry that they didn't watch me die. Now I will watch them. But first, Toi," Pleasura said to herself.

The guard came to her cell to bring her supper. She smiled at him and removed her clothes. She would let him have his fun until the time was right.

The island of Hondue had a new Queen now. She was very beautiful with her seven-foot frame and long golden hair. She came to them like a spirit. She kept peace and they prospered.

She vowed to them, to never, let Pleasura free, or ever allow an invasion again. As their Queen, Lori knew the time would come when she would also rule Rumora.

The End

About Mac Fortner

Mac grew up on the Ohio River in Evansville, Indiana. He lived in the Philippines and Vietnam for two and a half years while serving his country as a helicopter crew chief.

He writes songs in his spare time. That's where he got the idea to write his first book Rum City Bar. By adding suspense and humor to his songs–along with an intriguing plot–he has managed to write books you can almost sing.

Don't miss these books by Mac

Rum City Bar–Book One in the Sunny Ray Series

Knee Deep–Book One in the Cam Derringer Series

Find out more by visiting– www.macofortner.com

Made in the USA
San Bernardino,
CA